WILD POPPY

Philomena Blake and her identical twin sister, Patricia, have played piano duets together since childhood. When Patsy goes to New York, she suggests that Phil takes her place in a job she has just obtained, as teacher of music to Bryden Scott's children in Cumbria. Phil leaves London, certain that Mr Scott will not mind if she takes her sister's place. But Patsy has lied to Phil — Bryden Scott has no children and he does not need a teacher of music. But he is the most handsome man she has ever seen.

Books by Mary Jane Warmington
in the Linford Romance Library:

NURSE VICTORIA

MARY JANE WARMINGTON

$\blacklozenge$

WILD POPPY

Complete and Unabridged

LINFORD
Leicester

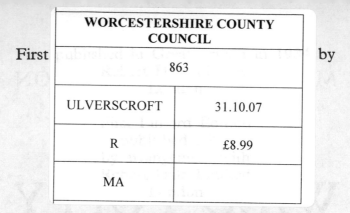

First Published in Great Britain in 1984 by

WORCESTERSHIRE COUNTY COUNCIL	
863	
ULVERSCROFT	31.10.07
R	£8.99
MA	

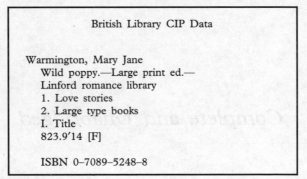

British Library CIP Data

Warmington, Mary Jane
  Wild poppy.—Large print ed.—
  Linford romance library
  1. Love stories
  2. Large type books
  I. Title
  823.9'14 [F]

  ISBN 0–7089–5248–8

Published by
F. A. Thorpe (Publishing) Ltd.
Anstey, Leicestershire

Set by Words & Graphics Ltd.
Anstey, Leicestershire
Printed and bound in Great Britain by
T. J. International Ltd., Padstow, Cornwall

This book is printed on acid-free paper

1

THE narrow brown road wound over the mountains and Phil Blake's heart beat nervously when the car engine began to labour. Gritting her teeth, she clung to the wheel until it purred more quietly as the road levelled out.

Thankfully she drove into a lay-by, then once again she spread out her map and began to look for Murdo Cragg. It was forty minutes since she had left Keswick and now this strange lonely road was almost frightening in its isolation after the busy streets of London traffic to which she was now much more accustomed.

Again she looked at the scrap of paper which her twin sister, Patricia, had given her and examined the scrawled but self-assured handwriting.

1

*'B. Scott. Murdo Cragg. Skelmor.
Cumbria.'*

Phil was now in the Skelmors district
and if she were reading her map
correctly, Murdo Cragg should be
roughly two miles further along the
road. She sat for a moment looking out
across the peaks to the towering heights
of Skiddaw, misty-purple in the pale
light of spring sunshine, and wondered
yet again why she had been mad enough
to come all this way because Patsy had
suggested that it was the only thing
to do. Fear and apprehension for the
future made her feel almost physically
sick, and she wound down the car
window and breathed in the cool fresh
air. Suppose this man . . . B. Scott
. . . did not want to offer her the job
he had already given to Patsy? Suppose
he saw that she was a different girl, what
would she do in that event?

"Of course Mr Scott won't mind,"
Patsy had assured her. "I mean, you
can teach as well as I can. We trained
together, played piano duets together,

and to be quite honest, Phil, you are a much better teacher than I. Now that Father has died, it's better that we split up. But in any case, we are so alike that Mr Scott will never spot the difference."

Phil had sighed. All their lives they had been managed by their father who had trained them to play piano duets. He had given them the best musical training possible, then he had dressed them alike, selected rather spectacular pieces of music for them to play and had found bookings for them, mainly in small theatres and cabarets.

But Arnold Blake had been a gambler and when he died there was little left for the twins. They did not even own a permanent home. Patsy could sing a little, and she wanted to join a Folk Group who were booked to appear in New York. She had fallen in love with Michael Todd, the leader of the group, and it was becoming increasingly obvious that she did not want her sister around.

But what was she to do? Phil had wondered, and for the first time in her life real fear had gripped her. She had never felt more lonely and vulnerable, not even when their mother died. She'd had her father then, and Patsy.

"You can always go to Cumbria and take on this job," Patsy had suggested, carelessly, handing her the piece of paper. "I landed it a few days ago before I knew Michael was willing to have me along with the Group. I forgot about it after that."

Phil read the scrawl with difficulty.

"What sort of job?"

"Teaching the piano, to Mr Scott's children."

"But . . . but he has given *you* the job, Patsy, not me. Why didn't you mention this before?"

Her sister shrugged. "I knew you'd be making a song and dance about it. Anyway, you could be me quite easily. Miss P. Blake. That could be Philomena as easily as Patricia. He only saw me for a short time. He will never know the difference."

"But where *did* you see him, Patsy?"

"Here in London, at an hotel. He had come up to London on business. He lives in the wilds up north, but you like that sort of thing, don't you?"

There was something dishonest about taking her sister's place, thought Phil, even if she knew she could do the job as well as Patsy.

"It's live-in, of course," Patsy added, "and you can have the car. I won't need it."

The battered old car was the only thing they owned. She'd had no choice, thought Phil, as she studied her map. The alternative was searching for a room in London and the fruitless round of looking for work. She and Patsy might have obtained engagements had they worked together, but she was not good enough on her own.

Phil let in the clutch then steered the car on to the road once more. The day had grown warm for early April and wild daffodils grew profusely in woodland areas. The bracken, burnt orange by the winter frosts, blazed like a flame against the new growth of grassland and in the far distance there were flashes of silver and gold as the sun sparkled on a distant lake.

Phil drove slowly, feeling almost sick with nerves even as her stomach rumbled emptily. She had eaten little for breakfast at Keswick where she stayed overnight, and she had not thought to buy picnic food. She had so little money to spare. Now she felt very hungry, but nerves also gripped her so that food might have choked her. Would she be offered lunch at Murdo Cragg?

She rounded a bend in the road, then saw heavy, wrought-iron gates almost directly ahead, one of which had been allowed to remain open. Leaving the car, she opened the other one, then drove along a narrow private road bordered with laurels and rhododendrons, at the foot of which were masses of daffodils in full bloom.

Suddenly the path widened and swung in a circle round the front of a house of such breath-taking beauty that Phil forgot her nerves and her hunger. It was stone built, its walls hung with Virginia creeper. It was finely-proportioned with many windows and on either side of the heavy oak door, flower beds were massed with daffodils and wallflowers. Phil had the choice of driving up to the front door, or round to the back of the house, and on impulse she chose the back of the house where the gravelled drive disappeared into a cobbled yard. There were many out-buildings and a horse had been tied up outside the stables. Phil was nervous of horses so she gave this one a wide berth as she looked for the back entrance to the house, then rang the bell.

An elderly woman with grey hair came to the door, and the smell of roasting lamb wafted out, making Phil's stomach feel empty again with hunger. Her young body was rebelling at the lack of food as she realised she had been eating very little over the past few days.

"Mr . . . Mr Scott, please," she said, nervously.

The woman eyed her searchingly.

"He's not here, Miss . . . "

"Blake. Philomena Blake."

"I'm sorry then, Miss Blake, but he is not seeing reporters at the moment in any case."

"I'm not a reporter," said Phil. "I'm here to start work . . . to teach, as you no doubt know. I'm . . . "

The woman's eyes went cool and she shook her head.

"Teach!" she echoed. "I'm sorry, Miss Blake, but that's not right. You young ladies try all sorts of dodges to see Mr Scott. Have you come from Keswick or Cockermouth?"

"London," said Phil, her face now scarlet with embarrassment. It was difficult to argue with conviction when it had been Patsy who had landed the job, and not herself.

"Truly I'm not a reporter, and I would not know why I was interviewing Mr Scott in any case. I'm a musician and I've come to teach the piano to Mr Scott's children."

"What children?"

Phil jumped with fright then whirled round as a very tall man with fair hair and bronzed skin walked towards her from the direction of the stables. He was wearing breeches, tall brown leather boots, and a fawn open-necked shirt, and he seemed to glow with health and vitality. As he drew nearer, Phil's eyes were rivetted on his face. She had seen him before somewhere. But where? . . . where? . . .

"You were saying something about my children?"

Phil's tongue ran over her dry lips. She did not like his tone or the look in his eyes as they ranged over her. This was not going at all as she had visualized. She and Patsy were so alike that she had expected to be welcomed in straight away as the new teacher, but this Mr Scott was looking at her with a stranger's eyes. Her body was beginning to feel so weak with hunger, however, that she had to try something.

"But, of course, Mr Scott," she said, covering her nerves with a smile. "Surely you must remember. I'm Phil Blake, and you engaged me to teach music to the children . . . teach the piano, that is, though I expect you would want them to learn the rudiments of music as a whole."

She faced him bravely, and slowly he came to stand in front of her.

"Nice try," he said, gently, "but it won't do, Miss . . . ah . . . Blake."

"Just what I've been telling her, Mr Bryden," said the housekeeper.

Mr Bryden! Then he was *not* Mr Scott. Phil breathed a sigh of relief. This must surely be the wrong man.

"I would like to speak to Mr Scott," she said. "It's Mr Scott's children I have come to teach."

"I *am* Mr Scott . . . Bryden Scott.

I'm . . . " he hesitated and glanced at the housekeeper, "I'm not married and I have no children, nor am I guardian to any child. I am sorry, Miss Blake, but you have made a mistake."

Phil's knees were beginning to shake. What could have gone wrong? Why had Patsy made such a mistake? At the same time she was realising why Mr Scott's appearance had been so familiar to her. He was Bryden Scott, whose television documentaries on British Wild Life had made very popular viewing. He had brought up a small family of red squirrels, and had written a book on the subject. Phil had read somewhere that Mr Scott was distressed because of the number of people who had travelled to his home in Cumbria merely to glimpse his attractive squirrels which were kept, as far as possible, in their natural habitat. No wonder he had not welcomed her visit.

"I'm sorry," she said, huskily. "I . . . I didn't realise who you were, Mr Scott."

He nodded then turned to his housekeeper.

"I'll attend to Roy, Mrs Cleland," he said, nodding towards the horse, "then I'll be in for lunch. Good-day, Miss Blake. Sorry your journey has been so unproductive."

He walked away and the housekeeper looked at Phil's white face with sympathy.

"He's not really a hard man," she said, gently, "but you see, his wee squirrel, Betsy, got killed when someone stepped on her after they had swarmed all over the garden. Some folk think that because they have read Mr Bryden's books and seen him on television, it entitles them to walk all over the place. They think he'll be out at the gate with the red carpet welcoming them. Well, he's trying to be quiet and write another book. I'm sure you understand, Miss. You're not like some of the young ladies . . . a bit on the strident side, if I may say so."

Black specks were beginning to float

in front of Phil's eyes, and she held out the scrap of paper towards Mrs Clcland.

"Isn't this Mr Scott's handwriting? It was given to . . . to . . . "

Suddenly Mrs Cleland's face began to whirl round in circles, and Phil slid to the ground in a dead faint.

2

SOMEONE was putting fiery liquid between her teeth, and Phil coughed and spluttered as she came to her senses. She felt sickly and light-headed and she was shivering violently even though a warm blanket had been placed around her and she lay on a long sofa near a huge kitchen fire blazing with logs.

"Where am I?" she whispered, then remembrance began to return when she saw Mr Bryden Scott sitting beside her on the sofa.

"You're still at Murdo Cragg, Miss Blake," he said, evenly, "and if you don't mind my saying so, you appear to be a very foolish young woman. When did you last eat? Where did you stay overnight?"

"Keswick," she said, rather feebly.

"Perhaps you are the type of girl

who prefers to go without breakfast? Well, it may do very well for London, but up here among the mountains, you can work up an appetite rather more quickly. Mrs Cleland! One more for lunch." He turned a severe eye on the girl. "You had better eat a meal with us before you set out for Keswick. In any case, I would be interested to hear how you came by this scrap of paper with my name and address written on it."

Phil wished she had enough strength to get up and leave the house immediately. She felt far from welcome and she did not like the look in Mr Scott's eyes as he looked at her steadily. Why had Patsy told her such a story if it was untrue? Sadly she was beginning to realise that her sister had sent her on a wild goose chase so that she could leave London for New York without argument. Yet Phil would never have stood in her sister's way.

"Is it your handwriting, Mr Scott?" she asked, feebly.

"Indeed it is."

"Then you gave it to my sister, my twin sister. She understood you had offered her a job to teach your . . . or someone's children. But Patsy was fortunate enough to get a job in New York and as we've always worked together, we . . . we thought you wouldn't mind if I came in her place. We . . . "

He was frowning, his face cold and hard as he studied the paper, then he looked closely into her face.

"We are certainly at cross purposes, Miss Blake," he told her. "On my last visit to London, a young lady whom I now recognise to be your twin sister . . . though you are not *really* identical, are you? . . . backed her car into mine, considerably damaging the paintwork. I now recognise the car as that rather unreliable heap which is parked in my yard. I hope your sister is well insured. There was no question of a teaching post. Did you say it was *music*, by the way? I find it all very confusing."

16

It had also been very confusing to Phil but with every word it was becoming more and more clear. Patsy had lied to her in everything. It would not be the first time, but this time she had enticed Phil into a situation which was so full of difficulties that she wondered how she was going to get out of it. She had hardly any money and she would need to return to London to look for another job. She had burned her boats by rushing up north, believing that all would be well when she arrived at Murdo Cragg. A job, which included food and shelter, would be waiting and she had rather looked forward to living amidst the beauty of the Cumbrian mountains.

But instead she had only found the ugliness of lies, and real fear for her future, made all the more frightening by the weakness of hunger and the prospect of the long drive south again in an unfit car. She would not even be able to sell it in order to have enough money to see her through the next few weeks. Who would want to buy such a car?

Shakily she struggled to her feet.

"I won't trouble you any further, Mr Scott. I'll go now."

His eyes narrowed. "Not until you have something to eat, Miss Blake. I don't want to find the police on my doorstep informing me that a blue mini has crashed near Murdo Cragg and that the driver's last port of call was this house."

She shivered. "Don't say things like that!"

"You are in no fit state to drive, also it seems to me that your sister has very strange ideas. You say you studied music together?"

Phil nodded. "We used to play piano duets. Our father arranged our training and managed to obtain bookings for us." She sighed a little. Their music was out of its era, though their father had always hoped that any day they would become popular once more. But he would never allow them to modernize their music, and their success had hardly been spectacular.

"And now?" he asked. "I'm still trying to understand why you are here."

"Our father died," she said, painfully. "There was very little left after all bills were paid, so Patsy and I decided to split up. She has gone to America with a Folk Group and . . . and she thought you wanted a teacher of music. I can only think she has confused you with someone else and has given me the wrong address."

Bryden Scott's eyes were sceptical and again Phil flushed. Mrs Cleland appeared in the doorway.

"Will you start now because of the young lady, Mr Bryden, or do you want to wait for Miss Delia?"

"We'll start now, Mrs Cleland. This way, Miss Blake. Can you walk or are you still light-headed?"

"I can walk, thank you," she said with dignity. "I . . . I'm most grateful for your hospitality."

Again he made no comment as they entered the dining room. Phil had an overall impression of a well-polished table, panelled walls, fine pictures and furniture and long crimson velvet drapes. But her hunger was great as she addressed herself to a small helping of soup.

"Moderation, Miss Blake," Bryden Scott advised. "There's plenty of time. Just eat a little and you'll soon feel better."

The soup, which Mrs Cleland called 'feather fowlie' was delicious and Phil had barely finished her first helping when the high light voice of a girl sounded outside the door and a moment later a very beautiful girl in riding habit hurried into the dining room.

"Sorry it took so long, Bryden darling. I'll never forgive Roy for throwing me into the beck. It's taken me ages to dry off. Oh . . . you've got a guest."

"Miss Philomena Blake . . . Miss

Delia Browne (with an 'e'), my neighbour," said Bryden Scott.

"How do you do?" said Phil.

If Miss Browne had been in the beck . . . did that mean brook, she wondered? . . . then it certainly didn't show. The tall dark girl was immaculately dressed. Her own pale blue suit felt crumpled by comparison, after her journey.

"How do you do, Miss Blake?" she was saying. "Are you here on a business trip? Don't tell me she's yet another journalist!" she said, turning to Bryden Scott.

"Miss Blake is a teacher of music," he said, smoothly, and Phil's cheeks became hot. She did not want this girl to know the circumstances of her visit to Murdo Cragg. She could imagine the derision in her eyes which had already raked her speculatively. By now she was well aware of Mr Scott's reasons for being suspicious of all visitors. It must have been very upsetting to lose his small squirrel and to have his privacy

21

invaded. Yet he was no longer a private person. He had sacrificed that when he made his first television film, and wrote his first book. He should be prepared to find himself an object of curiosity and speculation.

"Don't tell me you want to learn to play the piano, darling," Delia Browne was saying.

"It was Barbara's piano," Bryden Scott said, quietly. "I keep it tuned, of course, but I have no interest in learning to play."

Phil looked from one to the other, sensing undercurrents. Who was Barbara? Did she no longer play her piano? Ah well, it was unlikely she would ever find out. She looked at Delia Browne, thinking that her face seemed familiar to her as well as Bryden Scott's. No doubt she appeared in some of his films, or perhaps she was a horsewoman. A show jumper?

"I seem to be the object of much scrutiny, Miss Blake," she was saying lightly, as she refused Mrs Cleland's offer of potatoes.

"I'm sorry," said Phil, uncomfortably. "I thought I recognised you, that's all. Your face was familiar to me."

"Alas, I am a very private person. Bryden is the famous one, as you no doubt know. Are you making a long visit, Miss Blake?"

"I leave for London after lunch."

"Then I wish you a happy journey." Almost deliberately she turned to Bryden. "My parents are off to Madeira for a month or two, but Simon is coming home from London. It is time he returned home . . . don't you agree? . . . and helped Father with Highfield instead of running around with that rather arty crowd."

Simon . . . Simon Browne, with an 'E'. Phil had been given a small helping of chocolate mousse, but now her appetite had been appeased, and she was no longer hungry. Because suddenly things were becoming even more clear to her. Simon Browne was one of Patsy's friends and Phil was already familiar with the 'arty crowd' Miss Browne had mentioned. No doubt Patsy had obtained Bryden Scott's address from Simon. But no! . . . she had obtained it through her car accident, according to Bryden Scott. Her head began to whirl again. It was very confusing and more than anything she wanted to get hold of Patsy again and find out the truth. How, for instance, had she come to hit Bryden Scott's car in the first place? Phil did not believe in coincidences of this kind. There must be a tie-up somewhere.

"We will have coffee in the drawing room," Bryden Scott was saying.

"No, please, not for me," said Phil. Should she tell them now that she knew a man called Simon Browne and she suspected he might be Miss Browne's brother? She hesitated too long and the chance slipped away from her. In any case she only wanted to get away from this place. She felt, more and more, that she had no business to be accepting Bryden Scott's hospitality when she had no means of repaying it.

"I must be on my way, Mr Scott. It is rather a long drive back to London."

"All the more reason why you should fortify yourself with a cup of Mrs Cleland's good strong coffee. Besides, we still have business to discuss."

"In that case, I am the one to leave," said Delia Browne, lightly. "I must not keep you from your business. It's time I took my naughty Roy home."

She rose, a splendid figure in her riding coat, and smiled brightly at Phil.

"Have a good journey, Miss Blake. London, did you say? I often pop up to town myself for a spot of shopping. Clothes, mainly."

Her eyes swept over Phil who again wished she had chosen a more serviceable travelling suit. Now that Mrs Cleland's good, well-cooked food was doing its work, she was beginning to feel strength returning to her bones. She would listen politely to what Mr

Scott had to say, then she would leave as soon as possible.

After that . . . well . . . she was young and strong, and she had her health. There was no need to be afraid of the future.

Yet she was still shocked that Patsy could let her down in this fashion. As she watched Miss Browne's departure, Phil's thoughts were all for her sister. Patsy had always resented being born a twin. She said it deprived them both of individuality. Perhaps Patsy was right. Perhaps it was time to stand on her own feet.

3

"YOU pour," said Bryden Scott, pleasantly, as he conducted Phil to the drawing room where a large silver tray bearing a coffee pot with cream and sugar, had been placed on a small table.

"Cream and sugar for me," he added. "I like my coffee sweet."

"So do I," said Phil, ruefully. "Patsy says it will ruin my figure one day."

"No fear of that for some considerable time," said Bryden Scott, drily; "in fact you look like a young woman who has not been taking care of herself. And that's foolish, Miss Blake. That means you'll put your health at risk, end up in hospital and be a burden on the taxpayer . . . me!"

She flushed rosily. "I assure you, Mr Scott, that I do not intend to be a burden to anyone."

"Then I would like to know what you plan to do when you leave here, Miss Blake. I'm not unaware that you had expected to make a prolonged stay since I have seen the bags in the back of your car . . ."

"That is not your affair, Mr Scott."

"Oh, but I think it is. You expected food and shelter from me, also a situation teaching music. Now you know there is no such situation. I want to know what your plans are now."

"I shall return to London at once." It would cost her most of the money she had left, but she would worry about that tomorrow.

"You do realise that your road tax disc has run out . . . at the end of last month?"

She went pale. "Oh, no!"

Everything had been so confusing in London since her father had died. He had attended to all such details and it had mainly been Patsy who had used the car since then. She had forgotten to check up on such things.

"The police would take a dim view if you were stopped," he said. "What about your M.O.T?"

She nodded. The car would also need an M.O.T.

"Come back inside," Bryden Scott invited, kindly. "I think you need another cup of coffee."

Phil stood in the yard feeling more shattered than ever. All along she had felt that sooner or later she would be back in her own car, in charge of her own affairs again.

"I don't think you are very efficient, Miss Blake," Mr Scott was adding.

So much had happened in such a short time. She stared at him and to her horror she could feel a large hard lump forming in the back of her throat, and tears began to well in her eyes.

Mr Scott's expression grew grim.

"You had better remain here as my guest for tonight, Miss Blake. I have a dinner engagement but I am sure Mrs

Cleland will look after you. Tomorrow we will go into the question of your car. I have not forgotten that it put my own out of action for a week. I rather think we will have more to discuss in the morning."

"Couldn't someone drive me to the station?" she asked, almost desperately. She did not want to be beholden to this man.

"That would mean a drive to Penrith or Carlisle, not Keswick. Besides, what about your luggage? It's not inconsiderable."

Phil coloured. Always he kept reminding her of her presumption. And she *had* brought a few extra cases containing books and odds and ends from their old home which were precious to her, even though Patsy had said they were old-fashioned. She could not take them to London, however, without transport of some kind. And she would need to find new accommodation.

"Can you find this young woman a

room, Mrs Cleland?" she heard him asking.

This young woman! How . . . how impersonal that sounded. He managed to make her feel that she had been a great nuisance to him, as no doubt she was!

But Phil was too tired to argue further, and when Mrs Cleland came for her, she followed her gratefully up a broad stone staircase to a long landing with bedrooms on either side.

"I've put you in this wee room at the back of the house, Miss Blake," Mrs Cleland said, opening a door which led into a pretty room with blue sprigged wallpaper, pale blue bed quilt and soft rugs on a polished floor.

"It used to belong to Mr Bryden's Aunt Dorothy when she was a girl. She's married now and living abroad . . . Hong Kong, if you please. Anyway, I've put on the electric blanket and the bed will soon air for you. You can have your supper in the dining room later on, or up here if you like."

"I would rather have something simple in the kitchen with you, Mrs Cleland. I feel I've caused enough trouble already."

The housekeeper smiled. "Och, I like a bit of young company now and again and Mr Bryden won't eat you. He'll set you on the road tomorrow, but he'll want to be sure you are well equipped for the journey home. His young wife and baby daughter were killed on the motorway, you see. Mrs Scott was such a beautiful woman, and always out enjoying herself. She never thought to see to her car and Mr Bryden . . . I don't think he's ever forgiven himself for not seeing to her and baby Lee. She was such a quiet baby, too. Mrs Barbara . . . Mrs Scott, that is . . . was lovely to look at, not unlike Miss Browne. Tall and dark, and a great horsewoman. Maybe that's why she never bothered so much about her car. It was not in very good shape and the M.O.T. had run out . . . are you all right, Miss Blake?"

Phil had caught her breath as Mrs Cleland gave her this information. No wonder Bryden Scott had insisted that she remain at Murdo Cragg.

But she did not feel welcome in this strange house in spite of the friendly housekeeper. From her bedroom window she could look down on her battered old Mini with the rusting bodywork. Two of her cases had been brought up to the bedroom and the others, which proclaimed their contents as books and ornaments, still remained in the car.

On impulse Phil went along to the old-fashioned bathroom which Mrs Cleland had indicated. A bath and change of clothing might do her the world of good. She would rest and gather strength tonight, and she would worry about tomorrow tomorrow.

4

TO her own surprise, Phil slept like a log, only waking when Mrs Cleland tapped gently on her bedroom door and entered, bearing a small tray of tea. She unhooked the window shutters, folding them back so that the early morning sunlight streamed into the room.

Phil was awake in an instant.

"Oh dear, have I slept in?" she asked, throwing back the covers.

"Rest easy, child," Mrs Cleland said, soothingly. "There's no hurry. Mr Bryden goes out early in the morning, of course, because of the nature of his work."

"To see to his squirrels?" asked Phil. "I've seen documentaries on the life of the red squirrel, and I've read his book, which he called 'Betsy'. The photographs were wonderful."

"The wee squirrels are all dead," said Mrs Cleland sadly. "People used to come in their droves, walking all over the place to catch a glimpse of them. They had found out where Murdo Cragg was located, you see. Then one day Mr Bryden found wee Betsy lying dead, trampled by somebody's feet. The other two, Baldour and Selena died soon after. He was very upset, being so fond of them. But here I am, gossiping away when I have things to do in the kitchen. Come down when you're ready, Miss Blake, and have a good breakfast. Mr Bryden wants to see you in his room at nine-thirty. That was the message he left."

Mrs Cleland bustled out and Phil sipped her tea thoughtfully. How sad that the squirrels had died. No wonder Mr Scott did not care to have people calling on him out of the blue. He must grow tired of it. He seemed to dislike journalists. Was that because they probed into his private life and he did not care for that? Well, it must

35

all be in the past now. He owned this lovely house and he was not short of feminine company. Delia Browne and he appeared to be very close friends. Was he going to marry her?

Phil speculated as she searched in her bags for something more practical to wear, since she would have to return to London by public transport. She also counted out her money, wondering if she could let the car go to a scrap dealer. It might fetch a pound or two. And perhaps a mid-week single ticket to London would not cost such a great deal of money. That would leave enough to keep her for a few days until she found work of some kind . . . any kind, so long as it was legal and moral! And perhaps Mr Scott would be kind enough to take her to Penrith or Carlisle.

Once again, Phil preferred to eat her substantial breakfast in the charming old kitchen. There was a large scrubbed table in the centre of the room and a new shiny black Aga cooker took up half of the wall behind her. The door out of the kitchen led to the cobbled yard and beyond that the vegetable garden where an elderly man was already at work. Daffodils bloomed everywhere and a raspberry pink japonica was also in full bloom against the side wall of the house. Grape hyacinths contrasted with the daffodils and Phil was silent as she gazed out of the kitchen window at the beauty of the place. Everything was so quiet. Used as she was to London traffic, the peace of the place was quite disconcerting. She relaxed and began to enjoy it. Soon it would only be a memory.

Back up in her bedroom she repacked her bags into two manageable cases, and decided to ask Mrs Cleland to dispose of the third. Her books and ornaments were still in the car and she worried over what she could do with those. Perhaps she could send for them after she had an address to which they could be forwarded.

From the window she saw Bryden

Scott walking across the cobbled yard and whistling to his dog, a fine red setter named Shona. They walked into the kitchen and Phil checked her watch. Fifteen minutes later she descended the stairs and went along to the room Mrs Cleland indicated, knocking rather timidly on the door.

"Come in," he called, "and close the door properly. It works with a latch."

She did so, then came to sit down on the chair he indicated.

★ ★ ★

A number of letters had arrived in the mail. From her window Phil had seen the small red mail van driving into the cobbled yard, and heard the postman's cheery greeting as he handed in the bundle of letters. Now Bryden Scott was arranging them on his desk, which was not exactly tidy. An 'in' tray overflowed with papers and the 'out' tray contained a few copies of typewritten letters. Accounts and invoices sat about in small piles, weighed down by various paperweights. Mr Scott was reading one of his letters with apparent absorption. He glanced up at her.

"I . . . I'm sorry, Mr Scott," she began, "but I shall have to ask your help in taking me to Penrith. Or even Keswick. Perhaps I can arrange about the car when I've reached a town."

He waved a hand as though to silence her, and she remained silent, but uncomfortable. Again the room had a cosy, lived-in feeling even though some of the leather chairs were old and shabby. The walls had been washed chalk-white and sporting prints hung everywhere. Over the fireplace where a log fire again burned brightly, hung a portrait of a beautiful young girl with long dark ringlets and glowing cheeks. Unlike many portraits which Phil had seen and admired, this girl's delicate evening gown was of a more recent fashion and she had been painted with her head thrown back and happy laughter on her lips. A small name-plate had been placed on the frame at the bottom of the portrait, and Phil could clearly read *Wild Poppy by Gerard Fews*. Had this woman been Barbara Scott, Bryden's wife? If so, then why was she called 'Poppy'?

"I apologise for keeping you waiting," Mr Scott said, his deep voice breaking the silence so that she jumped a little. He looked at her levelly. "Your nerves are in bad shape, Miss Blake."

"I . . . I'm sorry," she said, huskily. "I'm just a little confused at the moment."

"As we all are," he said, heavily. "Now tell me again so that I may take notes. Your mother is dead? And now your father? What were their names?"

"I fail to see . . . "

"Names, please."

"Anthony and Claire Blake. British," she added a trifle tartly, and he smiled.

"And your sister?"

"Patricia. I am Philomena."

He looked up and smiled. "Nice name."

"I am always called Phil."

"Now, have you any other relatives? Aunts, uncles, cousins?"

She shook her head. "None whatever, apart from Patsy in New York, that is. No one." Her chin lifted a little. "I am responsible for myself."

"How old are you?"

"Nineteen."

He sighed deeply. "Can you do anything besides music? Can you type? . . . do office work?"

"I type, but slowly. I can't do shorthand. I used to help Father with his office work, but he insisted that Patsy and I put our music first."

There was a knock on the door and Mrs Cleland came in with coffee and biscuits.

"Joe Lundy had just called to collect the wee car," she informed them. "We've put Miss Blake's boxes in the hallway at the back entrance."

"Thank you, Mrs Cleland."

Phil half rose.

"What's happening? Where are my things? I . . . I don't think I want the car to be mended. I'll have to sell it . . . "

"*Sell* it!"

"As scrap. I won't get much, I know. Could . . . could I leave my books and other odds and ends here, then I will send for them and . . . and pay storage? I'll have to ask you to trust me."

"Wouldn't you prefer a job? I need an office girl. My secretary is at home at the moment. Her mother took ill about ten days ago and Miss Grant had to look after her. It would only be temporary until Miss Grant returns, but perhaps by that time the question of your car will be resolved and you can decide what you want to do. As you see, I need someone badly. I had hoped Miss Grant would be able to pop in now and again . . . she lives in a cottage on the estate . . . but Mrs Grant needs careful nursing. I must see if I cannot arrange help for her." He made a note on a pad, then placed it in the overflowing 'in' tray.

Suddenly he looked at her ruefully and Phil's heart softened. The hardness had gone from his face and he looked like a rather bewildered young man very much less sure of himself.

"If you had said you were a secretary when you first arrived, I would have thought it Divine Providence. Imagine my disappointment when you declared yourself a teacher of music . . . not that I've anything against music, you understand . . . but we . . . I . . . need someone . . . " He waved his hand over the desk.

Phil could feel the last of her doubts draining away. At first it all seemed too much of a coincidence. She had arrived here almost destitute, assuming she was going to do a job which had proved to be non-existent. Now Bryden Scott was offering her other work. Warning bells had rung in her head, but she could see that he really did need help.

"If you could spend a little time with

me explaining what you require me to do, then I could try to sort out some of the mess for you," she offered.

"Splendid. Now about salary . . . "

"No need to pay me if it is temporary," she said, quickly. "I would appreciate shelter, however, and food in the kitchen with Mrs Cleland."

"You shall have a salary," he said, clearly, "and you can pay for your car or do what you like with it. You will eat with me when I am at home. Other arrangements can be made when I am not here. Now, then, Miss Blake . . . Philomena . . . here is a pad and pencil. I am free until lunch-time. Let us sort out these letters."

★ ★ ★

It seemed strange to be living at Murdo Cragg, though as the days passed it seemed like the most natural thing in the world.

Bryden Scott helped Phil as far as possible with the correspondence, most of which only required an acknowledgement. She learned, however, that since the demise of his squirrels, his new television programme was in abeyance and new ideas were being considered, though here he waved a hand and said it could be discussed later. She felt that this part of his affairs worried him. Also he was due to start on a new book, but again, the few sentences he had put on paper had been thrown into the wastepaper basket, and the photographs which he had taken were jumbled up in a folder.

"I'll attend to those when I know what I want to do with them," he told her.

Often he would put on his duffle coat and tramp over the fells, and she learned that his hours were very erratic. Sometimes he would leave the house around dawn, and sometimes he would wander around in the night.

"He's had little peace since Mrs Barbara died with the wee one," Mrs Cleland said to Phil. "He was like one demented in the beginning, though he's better now. But it grinds away at him inside."

"I saw a painting in the study called Wild Poppy."

"It's what he always called her. She was dark with the colour of the wild poppy in her cheeks. She was a lovely girl was Mrs Barbara. Miss Delia is a fine-looking young woman, too, of course, but Mrs Barbara always seemed to want to be glowing, if you know what I mean."

"I know what you mean," Phil nodded. She, herself, did very little glowing these days. She would not ever be a wild poppy. With her fair hair and brown eyes, she could not be less like Barbara Scott. Yet she was beginning to feel more energetic than she had done for weeks and she was even putting on a bit of weight, which pleased Mrs Cleland.

"You aren't so much like a wee scarecrow now," she said, flatteringly. "Your cheeks are filling out."

"It's all those delicious puddings," said Phil, ruefully. "You'll have me as plump as a pigeon."

"No, just the corners filled out, that's all. Oh, I nearly forgot, Mr Bryden left a message for you to meet him out at the stables at ten o'clock this morning."

"The stables! Why the stables?"

"Maybe because he wants you to learn to ride."

Phil went pale. She was afraid of horses.

"Oh, no! I . . . I don't want to learn to ride."

"Sometimes it's easier to get about on horseback over this terrain," said Mrs Cleland. "I think Mr Bryden will want you to learn."

"I'm only here temporarily."

Mrs Cleland shot her a sideways glance and made no comment beyond saying she had passed on the message.

"You're to wear your jeans and anorak," she said, finally, "and I've got to find you a hat. There's plenty

47

about. Mrs Barbara rode a lot."

"I don't want . . . " began Phil again, then she held her tongue. She would argue it out with Bryden Scott.

He was talking to the groom, an elderly man with a weather-beaten face and the kindest eyes Phil had ever seen, when she walked over to the stables at precisely ten o'clock. She wore her jeans and anorak, but carried the black velvet riding hat under protest.

"You wanted to see me, Mr Scott?"

He turned and smiled at her, though she was in no mood to appreciate his more friendly overtures.

"Ah, there you are, Philomena. Donald Douglas has saddled up old Darby for you. He's elderly but very quiet and well-mannered. He'll do nicely for you to learn . . . "

Darby turned his head and he and Phil regarded one another without any sign of favour on the part of either.

"I'd rather not learn," she said, adding, "if you don't mind."

"Oh, but I *do* mind. You may want

me urgently one day when I am over the fells, and the quickest form of transport is the horse."

"I shan't be here long enough."

"We cannot predict how long you will be here," he said, equably. "Come on now, put yourself in Donald's hands, and you'll find great enjoyment in what he will teach you. Put that hat on. Let's just see if it is comfortable."

It will *never* be comfortable! thought Phil. She looked at Donald Douglas who had already shown her round the stables a day or two after she arrived, pointing out the attractions of the various horses and ponies, also the small trap which Barbara Scott had often used and with which she had won prizes at the Horse Trials.

"She was good with the pony and trap. She could turn it on a sixpence," Donald had said, proudly. "If there was a prize to be had, Mrs Scott would win it."

Had she ever ridden Darby? wondered Phil. But of course she must have!

Now she allowed herself to be helped into the saddle, sitting stiffly until Donald coaxed her to relax. Bryden Scott had retired into the stables, but soon he came out to watch and to offer encouragement.

"You're doing fine, Philomena."

She began to relax and to get the feel of it a little better. She opened her eyes instead of keeping them tightly closed and her breathing became easier. Suddenly there was the gentle sound of horse's hooves and Delia Browne rode delicately into the yard.

"Well!" she said. "What have we here? A new novice? Oh dear, Bryden darling, you *do* take on tasks at times. I thought Miss . . . ah . . . Blake was your new 'temp'. Does she have to learn to type on horseback?"

She laughed gaily and Phil's wavering confidence vanished completely.

"I've done enough," she said, sharply, to Donald Douglas. "Please help me down."

"*I'll* decide when you've done

enough." said Bryden.

"Oh, darling, allow the poor girl to come down. She doesn't look at all happy," said Delia, sweetly. "I don't think she's a horsewoman."

Phil did not think that Delia Browne was anything other than a horsewoman. She had never yet seen her dressed in any other type of clothing.

"Oh, very well," Bryden was saying irritably, "but only until ten o'clock tomorrow morning. Is that understood, Philomena?"

Delia Browne's eyebrows rose.

"Philomena? What a pretty name, Miss Blake. Can I beg a cup of coffee from you, darling? I'm parched. Oh, and I've brought an invitation to hounds. My parents have decided we must do something as soon as they return from holiday. It should be fun."

Phil listened as they walked towards the house, then she quietly turned away towards the back stairs which would lead to her room. She liked wearing something more businesslike while working in Bryden Scott's office. Sometimes people arrived to see him on business and she was obliged to receive them and to entertain them with a choice of drinks until Bryden could be located. She preferred to wear one of her suits or plain dresses for such duties, and she desired to change out of her jeans and sweater.

But Bryden Scott caught her arm.

"This way, Philomena. We'll all have coffee together in the morning room. Tell Mrs Cleland, then you can pour."

Phil hesitated, then nodded her obedience to his wishes, but she had no desire for more of Delia Browne's company. She did not want to hear about the proposed meeting of the local hunt. It appeared that Mr Browne was Master of the Hunt and that the role should rightfully belong to Bryden.

"You should take it up, darling," Delia was saying when Philomena, feeling self-conscious in her old jeans and sweater, joined them for coffee.

"Daddy is getting older, bless him, and Simon spends such a lot of time in London. He's been trying to do a bit of writing . . . for the theatre, you know . . . not like you, of course."

"I have never written a play in my life," said Bryden.

"I know that, darling, but you have written very successful books. Have you started your new one yet?"

"It's germinating," he said. "I'll need Philomena's help when I get going."

"Why don't you do one on fox-hunting?" asked Delia, brightly.

"Oh, no!" The words were out of Phil's mouth before she could stop them and they both turned to look at her. Delia's dark eyes were wide with astonishment.

"Don't tell me your are one of those crackpots who turn up with their banners at every Meet?" she asked.

"No, I'm not one of those," said Phil, uncomfortably, "but . . . but I can't pretend to like fox-hunting."

"I don't expect that you know

anything about it."

"Perhaps I don't," said Phil, "but I know that the animal is killed after being hunted until it is exhausted."

"You should see a hencoop after that same fox has been around," said Bryden. "I wonder what you would think then. Besides, it's the only way to get some of the foxes out of the fells."

"Surely not!" Phil's cheeks were bright. "Surely there must be a better way."

"They are cunning animals and completely unscrupulous. One of them killed three of our best hounds. It led them to the very edge of the fell, then dropped on to a ledge. The hounds couldn't stop themselves and hurtled over. That's the sort of animal you're defending."

Phil shuddered and Bryden Scott picked up his coffee cup, rattling it in the saucer.

"I've listened to this sort of argument since I can remember. It has the

54

habit of ending up 'evens', neither side giving way an inch, and each convinced in his or her own mind they are absolutely right. I would like more coffee, Philomena. What about your guest?"

Phil's cheeks coloured. "I apologise," she said. "I forgot to offer you more coffee, Miss Browne."

"Delia will do. You make me sound like a schoolmistress. And as for you, Bryden, surely I am not a *guest* in your home! Surely I need not be treated as a stranger here by one of your employees."

"Such was not my intention," said Bryden, smoothly. "I merely wanted Philomena to obey the courtesies and offer you more coffee. Would you care for another cup?"

"No, thank you, Bryden, I must go."

She rose to her feet, tall and statuesque, and beautiful.

"I'll telephone and give you all the arrangements about the Meet. It is

not finally decided yet. And Bryden!
. . . surely you won't miss *this* one.
I mean . . . time is going past now.
There is a lot of living to do."

Phil glanced at him and saw a hard
closed look on his face. Bryden Scott
must still love his wife very much.

"It's kind of you to take an interest,
Delia," he said, quietly. "I'll see you
out, my dear. You may go and change
now, Philomena. I want to see you in
my office ten minutes from now."

Phil nodded miserably. She had not
come out of this very well. She watched
Delia Browne slipping her arm into his
as they walked across the yard, and
a new emotion began to sweep over
her. She recognised it as jealousy, and
almost stopped in her tracks as she was
climbing the stairs. She was jealous of
Delia Brown! She did not want Bryden
Scott to be in love with her. She did
not want him to smile on her and show
her unexpected small kindnesses as he
did with Phil. She wanted all that for
herself!

She must be mad, thought Phil. Even if Bryden Scott was not attracted to Delia, he would *never* look at her. He was an important figure, a celebrity, and she was nobody. She was no longer even half of the Blake Twins who had achieved a certain popularity over the years.

But most of all, Bryden Scott would never turn to her. His Wild Poppy would always stand in the way.

5

A FEW days later everything began to change for Phil. She found that Bryden Scott was still in the breakfast room when she came downstairs and that he looked at her almost unseeingly when she walked into the room and wished him good morning.

"I shall type out that order to the grain suppliers this morning," she told him.

"Leave it," he said, tersely, "and don't come near the study for the next two hours. I wish to be there on my own. Afterwards there will be work for you to do."

He hurried off and Philomena heard the study door banging shut and she turned to Mrs Cleland.

"The mood is on him," the housekeeper said, rather sadly. "He'll have started his new book. Don't go near him until he's ready. After he's worked on it a wee while, he seems to settle down, then he's a bit more ordinary, but he's not himself till he's got it off his chest."

"But what will I do?" Phil asked. "Could I possibly go into Keswick and do some shopping? I . . . I've been paid and I want to see about the car and to buy a few odds and ends which I need."

"Take the pick-up. I don't suppose Mr Bryden would mind."

The Mini was a write-off. The garage mechanic shook his head mournfully and told Phil that it would have to be completely rebuilt in order to put it on the road again.

"It's full of rust," he said, "and it would never pass its M.O.T. What do you want to do, Miss? As I say, it could be done, but it would cost you quite a lot."

"That's out," she said, unhappily.

"I could sell it for you to someone

needing spare parts, if you like."

Phil was relieved. "I'd be grateful," she said.

"I'll let you know then, Miss Blake. I've got your telephone number. Mr Scott is a good customer of ours."

"Thanks," said Phil, dismally and turned away. Now her best means of transport back to London had gone for ever. She did her shopping then carried it to the car park where she had left the pick-up, glancing at her watch as she did so. It was time for her to return in case Mr Scott wanted her for work.

Phil deposited her purchases, then she was about to start the engine when she glanced at the car to her right. A young man had opened the door and had slid into the driver's seat. He did not see her, but as he turned to look behind him before driving out of the car park, Phil caught her breath at the sight of his face. It was Simon Browne who had been one of Patsy's friends in London. He had also been the one man who had got under her own guard and who had humiliated her almost beyond endurance.

Phil's eyes were dark as she drove slowly back to Murdo Cragg. She had never had much time for Patsy's friends whom she met regularly at a local pub. They were nearly all young people who had been connected with the theatre in some way, or to be more correct, *pretended* that they were connected with the theatre. She had liked one or two whom she felt to be genuine, worthwhile people, but she had felt uncomfortable with the others whose gaiety and wit had a touch of cruelty. She knew that they found it intriguing that although she and Patsy looked alike, it was her sister who was so full of fun and laughter and whose ready retort could cap every remark. Men flocked around Patsy, but she froze with shyness or sometimes distaste if they so much as touched her arm. She hated to be kissed if there was no affection behind that kiss.

At first Simon Browne had seemed

61

different. He and Patsy had become very close friends and she said that he had a style which the others lacked.

"Give Simon a chance to get to know you, darling," Patsy advised. "I don't want you to go all prickly on him, like a hedgehog. He no doubt sees plenty of those when he goes home to Cumbria. Try to be a little more friendly for my sake."

Phil did her best and next time Simon smiled at her, she returned his smile shyly and soon she was being included in their invitations. Then after a while, she found herself going out with Simon on her own when Michael Todd joined their crowd. He was certainly different from most of the other young men. His manners were well polished, though sometimes she sensed that they covered up an uncertain temper.

At first when Simon tried to kiss her, she had pushed him away.

"You're Patsy's friend, not mine," she told him, her heart thumping. No one ever wanted to kiss her when her sister was around. She could not stop the prickles from rising.

"I would like to think I'm a friend to both of you," he said, lightly. "You aren't frigid, are you, Phil?"

"No, of course not! It's just that I don't like being pawed about by someone who doesn't care tuppence about me but only wants . . . well . . . wants something for himself."

"Why couldn't it be something for both of us, Phil?" Simon had asked, softly. He had kissed her, then let her go, and that had broken up those prickles quicker than anything else might have done.

Next time Phil had accepted Simon's kisses and had begun to look on him more lovingly. He had played her as he might have played a fish in one of the local rivers, thought Phil with deep humiliation, as she drove out to Murdo Cragg. Life had suddenly seemed to be full of golden light and she had been happy for the first time since her father died.

Then she had overheard Simon and Patsy laughing immoderately and she had paused for a moment, before breaking in on them, in order to pick up a few coins which she had pulled out of her pocket along with her handkerchief.

"I should have passed around more bets," Simon was saying. "No one believed I could do it, but few women stand out against me, darling, and I knew it was only a matter of time with dear Phil. You've just got to apply a little psychology. Let her think about each step a little before it happens. She's not to be rushed like you, Pat dear. You like being swept along."

"Life's too short," Patsy had laughed, "and anyway, I've got Michael now. He's got a Folk Group together, did you know? they're very good. They're getting bookings. I had to get rid of you on to someone and I thought you'd find Phil a bit of a challenge. I thought, too, that she might be a harder nut than that. Daddy used to lecture us. Phil listened. I didn't. Been to bed with her yet?"

"Not yet. Give her time. Shall we put a bet on her asking me?"

"Done."

Phil had not waited to hear any more. She had felt physically sick and had crawled home and hidden herself away in a corner of her bedroom, then she had bathed in almost boiling water trying to wash away all contact with Simon Browne . . . with en 'e' as he liked to remark. She had been too hurt for tears, but gradually she had taken hold of herself and had decided on the best way to handle Simon. Next time they met, she had responded as usual to his overtures of affection, especially when he invited her to go with him to join their usual crowd at the usual meeting place.

"I want them all to see I've laid claim to you," said Simon, his eyes glittering. "I want them to know you're mine so that there are no predators."

Phil had gone along, and when

Simon put an arm round her in front of everyone, then pulled her close to him, she had turned round and kissed him lightly then she began to laugh almost helplessly. It was genuine laughter, born of her hysteria, and they had all stared at her, nonplussed.

"Oh, Simon!" she had said, after a while. "You are funny. Don't think I didn't see through you a mile away. I shouldn't be surprised if you weren't laying bets that you can get me into bed with you. If you have then . . . then . . . " again she had choked with laughter," . . . you can all collect from him, because he can't. I'm just choosy, that's all."

Simon's face had gone scarlet with fury and she was almost afraid for a moment when she saw the anger in him. She knew he would have struck her if the others had not been present.

"You little . . . little *nothing*," he ground out. "Do you think that I . . . I would even look at you? You're a nothing, a nobody!"

The laughter had gone and with it she had also lost a great deal of self-respect. Recently Bryden Scott had restored some of it as he watched his office being tidied and signed letters which had been carefully and competently typed. She had begun to feel like a person in her own right for the first time in her life. She was Philomena Blake, and not merely the quiet one of the Blake twins.

But now Simon Browne had come home to Cumbria. Was she likely to meet him at Murdo Cragg? Soon, perhaps, Miss Heather Grant would come back to work, and Phil would be able to return to London, away from Simon Browne once more. She did not want to breathe the same air as he! She would have to get away from Murdo Cragg. There was nothing to keep her there.

Except that once again her heart had been touched by a man. She had not wanted it to happen and, unlike Simon

Browne, Bryden had never encouraged her in any way. This time her greatest humiliation would be if he ever found out. She would feel so ashamed. Yet she had watched his kindness, and admired his wonderful talents. She had seen his television films and read his books, and although she was, indeed, a 'nobody' beside him, he had never made her feel that way. In fact, he had given her a new pride in herself and a new pattern for living. No longer would she tolerate anything trivial. From now on she would pursue excellence in every way. But she knew that when she returned to London, she would probably never see Bryden Scott again. And that was going to hurt. Mrs Cleland came out into the cobbled yard to greet Phil on her return to Murdo Cragg.

"Mr Bryden has been looking for you," she said, "though I said you would not be long. Is your wee car ready yet?"

"It's useless, Mrs Cleland," Phil

sighed deeply. "It's being sold for scrap, or similar. I'm going to miss it when I go back to London."

"Well, it seems like you've got work to do first. Mr Bryden has got the bit between the teeth and he's away. That Miss Grant always had a job keeping up with him when he got started."

"And I don't even write shorthand," said Phil, dismally.

She had eaten a light lunch in Keswick, but Mrs Cleland insisted that she sit down and enjoy a bowl of her good nourishing broth before Mr Bryden appeared again.

"I wouldn't go looking for him," she advised. "He'll have thought about something else and he'll be writing it all down before the thought has flown out of his head. He was aye like that, even as a laddie. Eat this soup, Miss Philomena. You're a bonny lass compared with the wee ghost we got from London, but you could do with a little more weight on your bones."

"Nothing will fit me," Phil moaned,

but her enjoyment of the soup was evident.

"Are you sure I shouldn't go knocking on the study door?" she asked, after all the washing up had been done. All her work was in the study. She could get on with her typing if only she were allowed to sit at her desk. "Can't I do *anything*, Mrs Cleland?"

"Maybe you could do some dusting in the drawing room, that's all. Everywhere else is clean and polished."

Phil sighed. She was not fond of dusting, but she was glad to do something. What form would the new book take? she wondered. She knew that his previous books had been about his squirrel family, but sadly they had all died. She knew, too, that until he had something equally absorbing to take their place, he had been unable to start a new book and that his television programme hung in doubt. As Mrs Cleland had confided, it seemed for a while as though everything was falling apart for Bryden Scott. He had lost his wife and baby daughter, also the squirrel family he loved. He must not also lose his work, thought Phil. It was exciting that he had started to write again.

She knew how he felt, she thought, as she dusted the pretty ornaments in the drawing room and polished the lovely old furniture. She felt the same about her music. She had been unable to put her heart into playing the piano after her father died and Patsy hadn't wanted them to play together. Patsy had taken to playing the guitar, however, whereas she was only interested in the piano.

She rubbed her duster over the shiny lid of the lovely piano, then lifted it and ran her fingers softly over the keys. Her desire to play had been dormant for so long, but now, suddenly, she could feel the familiar surge of excitement within her and the tingling sensation in her fingers when she knew she could play the kind of music which could give her deep inner satisfaction.

Sitting down Phil played the sad, heart-rending music of Schumann, then feeling soothed and rested, she forgot to play softly and launched into a sparkling étude by Chopin.

Suddenly the door was thrown open and Bryden Scott came striding into the room.

"What the hell do you think you are doing?" he demanded, thickly.

His hair stood up in ends all over his head, and his eyes blazed in a face almost grey with fatigue. Phil stopped playing abruptly and turned to him, her heart bounding with fright when she saw the anger in him.

"I — I'm sorry," she said. "I — I forgot the piano was not mine. I was playing one or two pieces . . . "

"You've spoiled all my best thoughts, that's all," he told her, his voice shaking. "I had it all in here, in my head. I've worked on it all morning in order to get everything down, but some of it would not come right. I even came to look for you so that we could type out what I had done, and work on it together. Then I saw where I had gone wrong — having found that you were unavailable, of course — and I have worked again to put it right and to keep hold of my ideas and thoughts. Then through the wall I hear nothing but crashing chords and musical fireworks. Chopin. *You* and Chopin! Now if you play this piano again while I am working, I will have to lock you out of this room. Is that understood?"

Phil was white to the lips.

"Yes," she said, "sir."

"No need for that. I won't be 'sirred' by you when I am not sure you use it with respect, but my wishes *will* be respected."

"Is Miss Grant ready to return to her job?" she asked very quietly. "Because if so, I would like to return to London."

He had been about to leave the room, but now he turned to look at her. She had again picked up the yellow duster and he sighed deeply.

"She is not yet ready to return, and for God's sake go and give that duster back to Mrs Cleland. I did not employ you as a housemaid. Go into the study. I have work for you to do there."

She hurried away without further protest and a moment later he had followed her into the study and closed the door.

"Do you want me to start typing your . . . your notes on the new book?"

"No, not yet. I have not yet licked it into shape. I'll give you plenty to type when I'm ready. Meantime these letters require answers, and I have signed cheques for these accounts. Enter them up in the book."

She worked as efficiently as she could, though she was too miserable to do completely competent work. How humiliating to be caught out like a naughty child, playing his precious piano. He had acted as though she had been playing 'Three Blind Mice' with one finger. Did he not understand that

74

she had been a professional performer, and although she could never aspire to being a concert pianist, nevertheless she was still better than most amateurs?

Tears stung her eyes and her throat felt tight. She made two typing errors, one after another, then with a small exclamation, she pulled the paper out of the typewriter and fed in a clean sheet.

"Leave that one until tomorrow," Bryden told her, almost impatiently.

"It's quite all right, I'm sure I can manage it," she assured him.

"No, leave it. Have you got a pretty dress, Philomena?"

She stared. "A . . . a pretty dress?"

"Yes, you know what I mean . . . something to wear for dinner in the evenings."

"Usually I change for dinner, but if my clothes are not pretty enough . . . " she began stiffly, then stopped as he waved a hand.

"Something to wear when you go out."

She thought about her coral silk dress with the swirling pleated skirt and the coral ear-rings which matched the colour exactly. She and Patsy had each received ear-rings on their eighteenth birthday, the only good jewellery they possessed.

"I do have a dress," she nodded, slowly. "Why do you wish to know?"

"Go and put it on. I'll book a table at Sharrow Bay, if they can fit us in, and give Mrs Cleland the night off."

"Where is Sharrow Bay?" she asked, carefully.

"Ullswater. You'll like it and they serve up food second to none. Come on, Philomena, don't argue any more. We've both had a tiring day and I think it's time we relaxed a little. Go make yourself pretty."

Phil rose and left the study as Bryden Scott picked up the telephone, though she did so reluctantly. Why was he inviting *her* to accompany him on an evening out? Usually he turned to Delia Browne for that sort of companionship.

Thinking of Delia brought Simon to mind. She dreaded meeting him again. He would be astonished to find her at Murdo Cragg. What would his reaction be? They had not parted exactly the best of friends.

Phil had had her soft fair curls cut in a short style which was easier to control than the long ringlets beloved by her father. He had worked very hard at keeping her and Patsy looking young and sweetly innocent. Their wardrobes had mainly consisted of frilly dresses in pastel shades, tied with huge bows at the back, and matching bows in their long hair.

After he died, Patsy had taken out their dresses and had burned them to a cinder, ignoring Phil's rather feeble protests.

"You know you hate them as much as I do," she said, firmly. "That part of our life is over, Phil."

"But we've hardly any clothes other than these," Phil had objected. "We might have been able to re-style them."

"Not a chance. We'll buy our own stuff. One good dress each . . . that's a must."

They had spent some of the money left to them on new clothes which each had chosen independently of one another. They had even avoided the same shops. But each had chosen jeans and sweaters, one or two suits and the 'one good dress'. Patsy had chosen plain black velvet with shoulder straps.

Now Phil showered and washed her hair, blowing it dry very quickly. It clung in soft feathers around her small face. Her wide brown eyes stared back at her rather anxiously, but the coral dress soon brought excited colour to her cheeks and as she clipped in her ear-rings, she knew that she had never looked better.

She picked up a cream silk shawl which had also been part of her wardrobe in the old days, and made her way downstairs.

Bryden was dressed in a plain dark suit with a white shirt and crimson silk tie. He looked like a stranger and she was suddenly very shy of him. What a strange quirk of fate had brought her to this lovely old house high up in the Cumbrian fells and to an evening out with Bryden Scott whose books were known to so many people.

He had glanced at her almost casually, but now he turned to look again.

"You look charming, Philomena," he said, and she coloured with pleasure. "Sharrow Bay can take us. Sometimes they do have a cancellation and can squeeze us in."

The clear crisp spring weather had broken into rain and high winds for a few days, but now those showers had died out and the evening was cool and clear as they drove into Keswick and took the A66 towards Penrith.

Phil had not yet explored the countryside very much. Her journey north through the Lake District had been fraught with anxiety and the beauty of the lakes and mountains had seemed to close in about her, but now with Bryden Scott at the wheel of his comfortable Rover, she began to relax and to admire the wonderful vista of mountains and rolling fells, a backcloth to the beautiful countryside.

Sharrow Bay Hotel on the shore of Lake Ullswater was a delight to Phil, and the warm friendly atmosphere made her relax and enjoy herself. For a short time they waited in the charming lounge until their table was made ready for them.

"I hope you're hungry," Bryden grinned. "You'll want to eat everything they offer here."

Phil thought about her snatched lunch in Keswick and the soup from Mrs Cleland. It all seemed to have been eaten a long time ago.

"I'm hungry," she nodded.

The menu offered such a wide variety of starters that she hardly knew which to choose but eventually settled for home-made pâté with steak for the main course. It arrived with so many delicious trimmings that her eyes popped, and the chocolate trifle which she chose for her sweet would long afterwards linger in her memory as the most delicious sweet she had ever tasted.

"We'll have coffee in the lounge," said Bryden after Phil had turned down all offers of after-dinner sweets, and they settled themselves into a quiet corner of the room with a wonderful view of the lake.

"Are you writing about another animal?" she ventured to ask him. "I mean, now that you have lost your squirrels . . . have you chosen something else?"

"I couldn't write about squirrels for ever more in any case," said Bryden. "That would have been stupid. No, I have been toying with the idea of writing a children's book."

His voice had wavered a little at the mention of children and on impulse she put a hand on his arm.

"Does it still hurt so very much, losing your baby daughter also, I mean?"

He looked out of the window and she sat back, chiding herself for being tactless and asking such questions. Then he sighed deeply.

"It's something I can't talk about, Philomena, not even to you. But it is one reason why I am angered when I see a car on the road which is not road worthy. Yours included."

"It has gone for scrap," she said, ruefully. "I have no transport now."

"And a good thing, too!" He looked at her and smiled. "If you are ready to go, I'll tell you about my new ideas for the book on the way home."

As she collected her wrap, she could only think that his hurt still went too deep for him to talk about Barbara. He must keep his Wild Poppy to himself, hugged inside his own heart.

When they walked out of the hotel to the car park, they found that the night was now very beautiful, with clear starlit skies and an almost full moon. The lake shimmered like diamonds in the moonlight.

"It's all so beautiful," said Phil, softly, as Bryden drove towards the A66 once more and turned the car in the direction of Keswick, and home. "At first I was almost afraid of such overpowering beauty, but now I can relax and enjoy it. London seems a million miles away."

"Yet you long for the place."

"Perhaps I did a little, at first. Not so much now, though I love London, too. I've had a letter from Patsy and she wants to stay in New York. I wonder how long that will last. She's inclined to be a wanderer."

"Ah, yes . . . Patsy," he repeated rather grimly, and Phil lapsed into silence. Bryden Scott had not yet forgotten the original misunderstandings which had brought her to Murdo Cragg in the first place.

"Tell me about the book," she said, quickly.

"It will be my first juvenile book," he said, "and if anyone thinks that writing for children is easy, I would like to disillusion them. I find it damned hard. However, it struck me that there might be a certain sort of . . . of . . . *adventure* in the way we live our lives on the hill farms for those youngsters who live out their lives in big cities. I thought I would do a year in the life of a boy who lives on one of the farms, from the time the lambs are born to the gathering of holly for Christmas. There would be the care of all the animals; not only the domestic animals, but the wild creatures which inhabit the fells . . . "

"Such as the foxes," said Phil, before she could stop herself, then wanted to bite out her tongue as she heard his small intake of breath.

"The foxes," he agreed, heavily. "They have their place like any other creature among our wild life."

She was silent for a while.

"It sounds as though it would make a

wonderful book. Many children would appreciate it."

"There would be illustrations, of course," Bryden went on. "I do my own work, as you know. My agent thinks this idea might also make a series of books, and that the idea could be put forward on television, though . . . " again he was silent, " . . . this might not have such an appeal for viewers. There are a great many wildlife programmes nowadays."

"And would that be important to you?"

He nodded. "Important, yes. I do not want to lose what I have built up."

"I understand," she said, softly.

He had stopped the car at the same spot where she had lingered when she first came to Murdo Cragg and together they looked out at the towering heights of Skiddaw, still slightly snowcapped, in the clear blue light of the moon.

"Philomena, I wish to say I'm sorry I stopped you playing the piano today.

I hope you will accept this evening as a token of apology. My wife used to play that particular piece of music. I expect it struck a wrong note . . . for me, that is."

"Oh, I *am* sorry," she whispered, wretchedly. "I didn't know."

"You could not possibly know," he told her. "I just wanted you to know that it was not your playing which upset me. You play beautifully. I should never have said those things, but it was a combination of trying to marshal my thoughts and hearing the music which Barbara used to play . . . "

"I'm sorry," she repeated. "It was entirely my fault. I should not have used your piano as though . . . as though it were my own."

"I hope you will play for me another time."

There was a lump in her throat. She could feel such pain for him at the loss of his wife and baby. Suddenly he put his arm round her and bent to kiss her cheek, but she turned her head and the kiss landed on her mouth. It was a light kiss, but a moment later Bryden Scott was holding her fiercely in his arms and was kissing her hungrily on the lips. She tried to push him away, then she relaxed, wanting him to hold her and to kiss her for ever. Her whole body tingled and her heart beat loud enough to suffocate her. She had never before felt such a surge of excitement rising within her.

Then as suddenly as he had kissed her, he was pushing her away and running a hand through his hair.

"I . . . I'm sorry, Philomena. That was unforgivable of me. I hope I have not frightened you."

Tears welled in her eyes and overflowed and immediately he cursed softly under his breath.

"I'm a fool. I did not mean this to happen," he said, reaching for a tissue. "Here, Philomena, dry those tears. No need to worry yourself. I'm taking you home now."

His voice was ragged and quietly Phil

dried her tears. She could not explain that they were caused by the sadness of knowing how much he still loved his wife. He had kissed her but at the time he probably imagined he was holding Barbara, his Wild Poppy, in his arms. Sadness for both of them wrenched her heart because she knew, now, that she loved Bryden Scott desperately and that, unlike Patsy, her love would only be given to one person.

But Bryden's love had also been given to one person, and she was now dead. How unhappy he must be.

He started the car and they drove home in silence. The house was quiet, Mrs Cleland having gone to bed, but the log fire still smouldered in the lounge.

"Would . . . would you like me to make you a hot drink?" Phil asked, hesitantly.

Bryden shook his head. "No, thank you. You may go to bed now, Philomena. It's getting late. I shall lock up. Oh, and there's no need to lock your door . . . " His lips twisted wryly. "I'm not that bad."

She hardly knew how to answer. She wanted to tell him that she was not offended by him in any way. She had not wanted his apology for kissing her.

"Thank you for the dinner," she said, awkwardly. "It was . . . was very memorable."

"I'm sure it was," he said. "Run off to bed with you. I shall expect you to work hard tomorrow. I shall have plenty of notes for you to type."

"Very well."

She walked towards the stairs then glanced back to where he stood in the lounge. He was looking at a large photograph of his wife and baby daughter, and Phil heard the clink of the decanter as he poured himself a finger or two of whisky. He must be feeling wretched, she thought, that he had let Barbara down. He must feel that he had betrayed his wife's memory, even though he had merely kissed Phil. Did he also feel this way with Delia?

But Delia Browne was the type of woman he might choose if he wished to marry for a second time. Barbara would no doubt approve of Delia as a second wife if her spirit still watched over Bryden. It would be different with Phil. She was different in every way from Barbara Scott, both in looks and background. In fact, she looked more like the baby, Lee, who was also fair like her father. Was that why Bryden had been upset? Was she too young to be kissed by him? Did he see her as another child?

Phil laid her hot cheeks on the pillow and tried to get some rest. Her dinner had been delicious, but it was more than she usually ate in the evenings and she was wakeful.

It was almost an hour before she heard Bryden Scott mounting the stairs. He stood for some time outside her door, then slowly he walked to his own room.

She could hear the door being closed gently.

6

PHIL'S interest was immediately caught by the pages which she had to type for Bryden's new book. When she had first arrived Phil had only been able to recognise that a sheep was rather different from a cow! Now she began to learn about the different breeds of sheep and which breed was best suited to the various farms.

Bryden had concentrated on Herdwick sheep and he planned to show the spinning and weaving of Herdwick wool and the fine hard-wearing garments which could be made up in good designs.

"We'll do a chapter on the care of the sheep during bad weather, also on the skill of a well-trained sheepdog," he decided. "Most people know that the sheep often have to be dug out of the snow, but I intend to give a detailed account of it. I think any young boy would enjoy reading about the bravery, endurance and sheer love of the animals which go into their care in the winter months. The weather is warm now, but you'll see what I mean when winter comes round, Philomena. By that time you'll be able to ride rather better, and we'll get out to some of the farms. You'll begin to know our neighbours a little better."

She nodded silently, though her thoughts were very busy. Had he forgotten that she was only here temporarily and that Miss Grant would soon be back to work as his secretary? Phil would not be here in the winter. Besides, she was making little progress with her riding, though she was no longer so afraid of the horses. Donald Douglas had said he was quite pleased with her though and Darby was now giving her a friendly nudge when she went out in the morning.

"That pony also pulls the wee

trap there," Donald Douglas told her. "When you get used to riding, we'll have you out in that one day. You might be good at it."

"No fear," said Phil, laughing. "I don't think I am a countrywoman, Donald. And yet . . . "

And yet there was something in her which responded to the beauty of the fells and valleys. She was beginning to love the peace and quiet of the place, and her eyes were becoming sharpened to the beauties all around her.

Now and again she went for a solitary walk along the banks of a small river which fed the Derwent, and she had paused with wonder and delight when she found a bank of beautiful sweetly-scented primroses in full bloom. At first she had wanted to pick all of them and to ask Mrs Cleland to put them in water for her so that she could appreciate their delicate scent in her bedroom, but she had paused after picking only one. They were so beautiful growing on the bank. Perhaps other people also enjoyed them.

Perhaps they should be left there in full bloom.

"Are you only going to pick one?"

Bryden's voice sounded behind her and she was startled.

"Yes."

"Don't you care for flowers?" he asked. "I've noticed that you don't even pick the daffodils."

"I think they should be allowed to grow," she said, "where they choose, and not where they have been dumped by someone who has picked them. They have their own roots after all."

He looked at her strangely. "Yes, I expect they have," he said. "Can you come and finish a report for me? I'm on the committee of the Civic Trust and there is a meeting tonight. I need to take it with me."

"Of course," she said at once. "I must have stayed out too long."

"Were you enjoying the out-of-doors, or hiding from . . . from anyone indoors?"

She laughed a little. "How could I

hide from Mrs Cleland. She always knows where I am. No, I was enjoying being outside. It's such heavenly fresh air. It makes me feel alive, as though all things were possible."

"Such as what?"

"Oh, I don't know . . . a feeling that the world is a wonderful place and I must not worry about finding a niche for myself when I leave here."

"Is it so important for you to go away to find that niche?"

She looked at him levelly. He did not understand. His roots went deep, much deeper even than the primrose she had newly picked. He did not understand that she no longer had any roots and was only one step removed from living in a tent at the side of the road.

"Yes it is," she nodded, and he sighed a little.

"Let me see the primrose," he said, and she handed it to him.

"My wife was like a wild poppy," he said, and it seemed to her that there was great sadness in his voice, "but you are like this primrose. She was so dark yet you are fair."

He twirled it round in his fingers, then marched away from her and into the house.

The primroses would be dead when the wild poppies came into bloom, thought Phil, as she made her way to the study. She thought they were beautiful flowers, but others might find primroses colourless. Was that what Bryden Scott had meant . . . that she was colourless?

She tried to tell herself it did not matter. Yet it did, very much.

★ ★ ★

Having made friends with Darby, Phil began to be a little more adventurous when she went out riding and to make small excursions of her own over the fells. Bryden had sometimes taken her along with him in his car when he went to talk to the farmers, or drove into Keswick or Cockermouth to visit the post office and shop for necessities. But the terrain was still fairly strange to her.

Delia Browne called to see Bryden quite regularly and sometimes he would leave a message with Phil that he would be at Highfield if anything urgent turned up. It was then that she would experience the depressing and, to her, shaming feelings of jealousy. She was beginning to love Bryden Scott more and more each day, loving him in spite of his moods. He could be full of gentleness and compassion, then he would sometimes be roused to anger if he thought someone was being stupid and obstructive towards him.

He found a baby owl which had tumbled from its nest high up in the barn and he fed the tiny creature, then encouraged the owl to live in the wild again when it was old enough to be independent.

"Couldn't you put it back in the nest?" Phil had asked, and Bryden had quietly shown her the location of the nest.

"How?" he asked. "How do I get up to that height? Besides, it has taken a tumble. It's a miracle it isn't dead. The poor creature needs care. I had a similar experience with a kestrel chick, but the kestrel was easier to train than the owl and from past experience, this one will be difficult to put into the wild when it is old enough. I shall have to let the authorities know, of course. Wild birds are protected, and rightly so."

"Aye, and if you bring eagles and buzzards home, I'm leaving here, Mr Bryden," Mrs Cleland told him, darkly. "When he was a wee boy it was mice and frogs. He has frightened the life out of me many a time."

Bryden grinned and Phil could see the small boy in him again, and loved him the more.

That evening after dinner he had asked Phil to play for him and she had been circumspect about it. She had been carefully avoiding all contact with the piano, allowing Mrs Cleland to dust it and to clean the keyboard. Now she hesitated.

"What's wrong?" he asked. "I'm not working now. I would like to hear you playing again."

"What would you like to hear?"

"I leave it to you."

She played one or two pieces by Scarlatti then Grieg.

"What did you play on the stage?" he asked.

"I'd prefer not to play any of that," she said. "Father liked 'Busy Fingers', and the 'Bees Wedding', and 'Nola' . . . that sort of thing. You know what I mean? Patsy and I hated it."

"Play 'Nola'."

Reluctantly she did so and he sat in his chair by the fire, smoking his pipe. Then she played softer music, ending up with 'Clair de Lune'. She would have to get to know what he *really* liked.

When she finished playing 'Clair

de Lune' she looked over towards his chair, seeing that his head had slipped sideways and his eyes were closed. Carefully she walked over and removed the pipe from his fingers. Then she bent down and lightly kissed his forehead. Immediately his arms were wrapped round her and he held her close, then he kissed her.

"I . . . I thought you were asleep," she whispered.

"The Sleeping Beauty in reverse," he grinned, "where the beautiful princess wakes up the beast."

"The prince," she corrected. "The prince found his way through a hedge of prickles."

"I must find out how he did it." He sighed and moved in his chair. "Where did you put my pipe, Philomena?" he asked, and suddenly anger began to stir in her. How dare he keep on kissing her when he did not really mean it! She was only a substitute for Delia Browne. He was always going over to Highfield and sometimes he came home very late.

"'Where the damn are *my* slippers, Eliza?'" she quoted, her eyes glinting.

He laughed heartily, then he sobered.

"Are you quite sure you have no relatives? Beyond your sister in New York? Did your parents not have any brothers or sisters?"

"My mother died when we were young. I don't think she kept in touch with her own people. We had an uncle who came once to see us, but he and Daddy had a row, as I seem to remember. I think he was probably our only relative at that time. I don't know if he is still alive. Is it important?"

"Don't you *want* to find out if you have any people of your own?"

Apart from her father and Patsy, Phil had got along without relatives for most of her life.

"Not particularly," she shrugged. "I might be an intrusion into their lives."

"What was your mother's maiden name?"

"Somerville. Anne Somerville."

"And do you know when your

parents were married?"

She gave the date, then she frowned.

"I don't understand why you want to know all this. Do I need security clearance or something?"

"No, nothing like that," he told her, smiling a little. "But you are very young to be without relations, except for your sister, that is. I'm only thinking about the future."

"I'm used to that," she assured him.

It was only later that the full implication struck her with regard to his desire to find a family for her, and when it did, pain filled her heart again. She was like the small birds he had found and cared for until they were well again, then he pushed them back into the wilds as soon as he was confident that they could survive in their own environment. To Bryden she was like one of those small birds. He had fed her and cared for her, given her work to do and money to buy a few new pretty clothes. Now he sought to push her out of the nest and back into her own environment, but he always had to be sure that his weak creatures would survive thereafter. He wanted to find an older relative for her, one to whom he could hand her over with a good clear conscience. Phil's heart stabbed with pain, but after a while anger and pride came to her rescue. From now on Bryden Scott was going to be left in no doubt that she could take care of herself.

7

RIDING Darby became an early morning habit with Phil as part of her scheme to become self-sufficient, but one morning when she walked over to the stables, she found a pony harnessed to the dainty little trap and Phil exclaimed with pleasure.

"Oh, how pretty!" she said to Donald Douglas. "It's like something out of a story book, or another age. Somehow it makes London Traffic seem a very long way away."

"Would you like to try it?" he asked.

This time Phil had no hesitation.

"I would," she agreed and Donald began to teach her the difference between riding a horse and managing a horse and trap.

"That will do for today," he said at the end of her lesson, "but, by Jove, Miss Philomena, I think you're a natural. Given patience and practice, I could train you up to take a prize at the Horse Trials."

"No fear," laughed Phil. "I'll never be that good, though I quite enjoyed learning to manage the trap."

"You've done very well," said Donald Douglas.

"I'm not afraid of old Darby any more," said Phil. "We're friends now."

The following morning she ventured further on Darby than she had ever done before. Spring had passed into summer and the mornings were clear and bright, the air warm and soft with the promise of a fine day.

Phil's spirits rose. Aided and abetted by Mrs Cleland, her body had grown stronger with the good food served up to her, and the exercise and fresh air had brought a soft glow of colour to her cheeks. Her hair clustered in soft fair curls about her cheeks and she felt very fit and full of well-being.

In a short while she would return to Murdo Cragg and begin work with

Bryden on the new book which was fast becoming as fascinating to her as it was to him. Her typing had improved and she was also trying to learn shorthand.

"It will be a help to me when Miss Grant returns and I have to get another job," she explained to Bryden.

He had seemed rather taken aback and had stared at her thoughtfully for a long time.

"Don't you miss your own career?" he asked. "Wouldn't you prefer to be an artist rather than a secretary . . . especially if further training could be arranged for you?"

"That would be out of the question. I'm not good enough. I'll never be good enough for the concert platform even if I could afford more training, and I don't want to do light entertainment on my own. It wasn't so bad with Patsy, I suppose. At least we appealed to a certain section of the public."

"Do you miss your sister?"

She shrugged. "Sometimes. We were

not really as close as twins are supposed to be. We were very different from one another at heart."

Now she thought about Patsy as Darby delicately picked his way over rough ground on top of the fells. She had written several times to her sister but had received few letters in return. That did not worry her. Patsy was always meaning to get down to doing things, but always something turned up to occupy her time, and there was never enough hours in Patsy's days. She must be well and happy, thought Phil, or she *would* have heard from her.

"We've come far enough, my boy," Phil told Darby. "No cropping grass by the side of the road either. Home for us, then I have work to do."

She turned away, then twisted round when she heard the sound of another horse behind her, and a moment later she recognised Delia Browne's black horse, Roy. But the rider was not Delia; it was Simon.

Phil's heart leapt, then plummeted.

Almost without realising it, she knew she had been keeping herself as far removed from Simon Browne as possible. She had no wish to be reminded of those days in London when she seemed to have lived on the fringes of Patsy's life, never her own. She must have been a dull young woman in those days, she thought, but it had been no excuse for Simon Browne. He should not have taken advantage of her innocence.

Phil wanted to spur Darby into action and to see how fast they could go on the return journey to Murdo Cragg, but she had no wish to allow Simon Browne to guess how badly he affected her. It would only encourage him to amuse himself again at her expense.

Instead she waited patiently until Roy was brought to a halt beside her.

"Well, well, if it isn't little Philomena," he said, smiling, though she saw the speculation in his eyes. "I've been meaning to call on you at Murdo Cragg, but I understand from Bryden that you are a working girl now. I could not disturb the typist at her labours. How are you, Phil? As a matter of fact, you look fabulous."

"Thank you," she said, quietly.

"It's strange how things turn out. I believe you came up to take over a teaching job from Patsy . . . teaching Bryden's children! She's quite a girl is your sister. Very inventive. When one scheme does not work out, she can soon invent another."

"I've really got to get back, Simon," said Phil, then she paused.

"What scheme?"

He grinned. "Getting herself a little extra money for her trip to the U.S. of A. I spotted Bryden's car outside his favourite hotel in Kensington when she was giving me a lift and showed it to Patsy. She was so busy looking that she hit it, then thought she ought to cash in on the accident. He had parked it badly, as usual. Only it did not work out that way. For once her big brown eyes and pretty curls let her down and even a few heart-breaking tears had no effect. Bryden would not play. Instead they exchanged addresses and Patsy said a few naughty words to me when we got back to the flat. I don't think she gave her proper address either! I was very much amused when I heard from Delia that you had turned up at the Cragg. What happened? I should have expected Bryden to kick you out as soon as he set eyes on you. He's such a supercilious creature and he must have thought you were out of your mind when you said you had come to teach music! That was a corker!"

"I don't want to discuss it," said Phil, her cheeks now flaming with colour. It had been bad enough with Bryden, but now it was even worse listening to how much Simon had been amused by Patsy's lies. She would have something to say to her sister when she saw her again!

She listened to him rambling on. He had not changed, she thought. He was still the same Simon Browne whether he was clad in jeans and sweater, or in a good tweed coat and riding hat as he was this morning. Now he was telling her things which she had only vaguely guessed, and which madc her feel humiliated beyond words. She felt even more embarrassed about going back to Murdo Cragg to do a day's work with the truth behind Patsy's possession of Bryden Scott's address now fully explained.

Often she had wondered how Patsy's car accident had happened, and now she knew. And her sister had tried to get money out of Bryden because of it! How could she be so dishonest? Patsy often did very stupid things at times. She never stopped to think.

And Bryden must have known that Patsy had tried to get money out of him, yet he had taken *her* into his home, and had given her a job. She felt the warmth of embarrassment sweeping over her again. She was certainly one of his lame ducks.

"I must get back, Simon," she said,

and turned away towards Murdo Cragg. He rode beside her, his mocking eyes resting on her.

"As a matter of fact I've been looking out for you, Phil," he told her. "I've been exiled up here away from London for a while. Economic reasons. I was given an allowance when I first went to London, but no longer. We won't go into that for now. But one or two projects have not been so good and only because of the Recession. If it had not been for the damned Recession, Simon Browne's name would be a household word. I've written rather a good play but no one will take it on."

"Sad for you, Simon."

"Instead I'm forced to return to Highfield while the parents are away, and help Delia to run the place. She likes the life. I don't. I won't be happy until I get back to where it is all happening, but I'll have to put up with it now. And my guess is that you are in the same boat until Patsy returns, only you have to eat, Philomena. That's it, isn't it? You are such an innocent when that Patsy is around, and I expect that after she got rid of you up north, she made off with your money as well as her own. She'll have diddled you out of it. I asked her to stake me for one small pressing bill after your affairs were all sorted out, and she wouldn't yet I helped her once. Oh, she paid me back, and I would have paid her but she is mean. She's really mercenary."

His mouth twisted into sulky lines.

"Anyway, here we are, both of us, Phil darling. We can entertain one another. When are you free? Shall I call for you this evening? There isn't much to do up here, but we'd find something. There are plenty of local girls, of course, but I can't talk to them about old times. I'm lonely, Phil."

They had ridden into the yard at Murdo Cragg and Phil's face was white as she dismounted.

"I don't think so, thank you, Simon," she said. "I don't have to remind you that you were Patsy's friend, never mine."

He, too, dismounted and caught her arm. Donald Douglas had come forward to lead Darby away, and Phil paused as Simon Browne held her firmly.

"Oh, I think you have been my friend, too," he said, softly, "and I don't need to remind you that Patsy is not around. She's in New York. She's gone off with that hound, Michael Todd, and I have to confess that I miss her. I really miss that girl. You're the next best thing. At least you look alike."

She went pale with anger at his tone.

"Leave me alone," she said, her voice shaking. "I don't want anything to do with you."

"Too bad. You're going to have to put up with me while I'm here, otherwise I might find life a bit dull."

"Philomena!"

Her name was rapped out loudly

and she jumped with fright. Bryden had appeared from the direction of the house and from his expression he was not in the best of moods.

"Hello, Browne," he said, evenly. "You're rather early for visiting hours unless it's urgent."

"I'm not visiting," said Simon with a bright smile, "so you can put away the warm welcome and the hospitality. I merely brought Philomena home. We're old friends, you know."

Bryden Scott's eyebrows rose.

"I did not know. You said nothing about that when you met Delia, Philomena."

"I . . . I wasn't sure that Simon was Delia's brother," said Phil, lamely, "and in any case, he's Patsy's friend, not mine."

"Oh, come on, Phil, that sounds very ungracious," said Simon easily. "You know very well I'm a friend to both of you. How else would you have known about Bryden and Murdo Cragg? But I mustn't hold up the good work. I have my own daily grind ahead of me. I'll call for you around seven."

She began to shake her head. "Simon, I told you . . . "

"Yes, but I'm sure Bryden won't work you so hard that you can't go out with an old friend. She *does* get time off, doesn't she?"

"Of course," said Bryden, stiffly.

"There you are then. Seven o'clock. See you!"

He swung back into the saddle and Roy cantered off leaving Phil feeling angry and frustrated. She had no wish to go out with Simon Browne, yet he and Bryden seemed to have arranged it all very nicely between them.

"So you *did* know about Murdo Cragg before you came here?" he asked her, harshly.

Her face flamed. "I did not! It was just as I told you. It was — "

"Yes, I know. Patsy. The friend of Simon Browne. But you are here and not Patsy, and he is taking you out this evening. How nice for you. Go and eat a meal, then I'll see you in the study when you're ready."

"I only want coffee."

"I said to eat some food. There is time enough for that."

Normally Phil brought a healthy appetite back from her morning ride, but this morning she only wanted toast and coffee, whatever Bryden directed. She felt very miserable and suspected that Bryden thought she had been lying when she first came to the Cragg. But at least she was in charge of her own stomach, she thought resentfully.

"He's had a letter in the post which upset him," Mrs Cleland informed her.

"Oh dear." It might have been about his new T.V. series, she thought. If it had not been approved, he would be like a bear with a sore head and she would have to put up with him all day, then Simon Browne in the evening.

"You look down in the mouth yourself," said Mrs Cleland.

"Do you know Simon Browne?" she asked the housekeeper.

"Oh, aye, I know him," said Mrs Cleland, and there was a decided drop in temperature. "Time was when he was never away from here, and he was a cheeky young fellow. I've had to keep my temper with him many a time. I'm not one to gossip, though . . . " she paused and cut up some bread vigorously. "I think he went off to London in a quick hurry. His father would be glad to get him out of the road likely. Once he gets into scrapes old Mr Browne soon gets him away. Fair spoiled he was, and a spoiled boy makes a spoiled man. Have you only just met him, Miss Philomena?"

"No, I met him in London. He . . . he wants me to go out with him this evening for old time's sake."

There was heavy silence while Mrs Cleland decided that the sink tap needed vigorous wiping.

"Are you going?"

"It seems I have little choice."

"Surely you can please yourself, and please yourself you will! You've a mind of your own, Miss Philomena. Will you be wanting more coffee?"

She shook her head and rose from the table. Could she please herself? she wondered. Simon was very good at making a scene if he did not get his own way.

But more than that was this information he had given her about Patsy. How could she do such a thing! How could she try to get money out of people? Until their father died, they'd both had an equal allowance, but Patsy's never seemed to last. She had spent most of Phil's as well as her own which was one reason why Phil had had an ill-equipped wardrobe. Most of the money she now earned was being spent carefully on pretty clothes, mostly good and sensible, and her wardrobe was now better equipped than it had ever been, and her appearance all the better for that. She had not liked the way Simon Browne's eyes had lingered

119

on her. She was going to have trouble with him, she thought disconsolately, just when she thought she had rid herself of him for ever. She cringed when she thought of her own naïvety when she had imagined herself in love with him, and how hurt she had been when she found out he was laughing at her all the time. He should never have had the power to hurt her.

"So there you are!" said Bryden when she walked into the study. "Could you reply to these letters? I've put notes on all of them as to what I wish to say. And here are the manuscript notes for you to type. I have to go to Carlisle today. It had been my intention to take you along, but we would not be back in time for you to keep your date, so you had better remain here."

"I have no wish to keep that date," said Phil, swiftly.

"Then you should not have made it. I will see you when I get back."

He was gone in an instant and Phil was left with the sheaf of letters in her hand. A quick leaf through them showed her that they were not important. She could easily have done them the following day, and caught up with her typing of the book. And she would have loved to go to Carlisle. She would love to have wandered round the bigger stores if Bryden could have spared her for an hour. It was really very unfair of him, and very childish, she thought, resentfully. He *and* Mrs Cleland had made it very plain that Simon Browne was not exactly popular at Murdo Cragg, and Simon had made it equally plain that he intended to seek out her company when he felt bored at Highfield. Surely there must be some attractive local girl who could keep him amused she pondered. He would have to marry one day and men like Simon Browne often married girls from their own background.

Phil sat down to type out the letters. She felt uneasy and some of her inner joy and contentment had vanished, even though Mrs Cleland had recovered her good temper when she brought in Phil's lunch.

"Donald Douglas had an hour off on the river and caught a couple o' wee trout," she said. "I thought you might enjoy them for your lunch."

"Oh, Mrs Cleland! I would!" said Phil. She felt hungry after having skimped breakfast. "Did we have any more post this morning?"

"No, just that one letter for Mr Bryden. It didn't please him."

He had not mentioned it to her. She sighed, thinking that she was becoming too much involved in Bryden's affairs.

★ ★ ★

The afternoon dragged endlessly and by six o'clock Phil was almost glad that she was going out for the evening. Simon could be fun sometimes, and she could soon deal with him if he became objectionable.

She changed into her best silk dress, the one she had worn when going out with Bryden, taking more than usual care with her appearance.

"My, but you've grown into a bonny young woman, Miss Philomena," said Mrs Cleland, admiringly. "The good weather has put nice colour on your skin. You look really well."

"Does 'bonny' mean fat?" Phil asked.

"Not in Scotland where I come from and you've a long way to go before you're fat," said Mrs Cleland whose own ample form did not trouble her in the least.

Simon drove up a short time later and his eyes narrowed when he looked at Phil. If only he could break up that cool, rather icy exterior which she presented to him these days, and return to all that warmth, and love, which she had shown for him at one time, she would be even more worthwhile than Patsy who had shown very poor taste in preferring Michael Todd to himself. Phil had more style, more integrity, and more self-respect. All in all she was the more beautiful of the two girls.

"You look wonderful, Phil," he said, generously, as he helped her into his car then climbed into the driving seat. Leaning over he kissed her on the lips and Phil coloured angrily, aware that Mrs Cleland was watching from the window.

"Leave me alone, Simon," she said. "You asked me out, but you'd better know how we stand. I'm coming with you, but not happily. You appear to be determined to take me out for the evening but you would have been well advised to ask another girl."

"And maybe you should understand something, too, Philomena," he said, his eyes glinting as the car shot up the drive to the main road. "Practically every girl of marriageable age in the county would fall over backwards to go out with me. *And* I mean that literally. Highfield is one of the finest estates in the neighbourhood. It will be mine one day. Maybe I look like a member of the usual crowd in London, but in this county I am Simon Browne, and I intend to be treated with respect, especially by . . . "

"By a mere typist," finished Phil. "Go on say it. You might as well. I shan't be offended in the least. Nor shall I be offended if you find one of those local girls to console you. I'm quite sure you won't have to look far to find one who is as beautiful as any man could wish. As for me, *I* like to have respect, too. Remember that."

She could sense his anger, then suddenly he turned to her and began to laugh.

"What a way to start a date, wrangling with each other! That's what I remember about you, Phil . . . those thorns which keep all comers at bay. It's much more fun to try to break through them to that lovely soft amenable girl I remember. That's why I want to take you out rather than anyone else. You know we could have a very good 'meaningful relationship', if only you'd be willing."

"I don't like being led up the garden, then having people laugh at me behind my back," she said, recklessly, then she could have bitten out her tongue when he turned to her, suddenly enlightened.

"Oh, so *that*'s what happened!" he said, softly. "You overheard my conversation with Patsy! Then you pretended you'd been making fun of me! It angered me that I had not spotted it."

"How do you think *I* felt?" she demanded, hotly. She was furious with herself for allowing him to know the truth, yet what did it matter now? It was all in the past and she had no more illusions about Simon.

They were driving along a winding road by the side of Lake Bassenthwaite and Phil looked at the sun sparkling on the lake.

"Let's forget the past," said Simon. "I've booked a table at the Pheasant. Just let's enjoy ourselves this evening."

"With no strings?" she asked.

"If that's the way you want it."

"I'd rather have a quiet evening without emotional stress, if you don't mind," she said. "It hasn't been the best of days."

"Okay then, that's how it is going to be."

Phil loved the Pheasant on sight and Simon led her into the charming lounge where a log fire burned brightly and a long-haired black cat rose and walked towards her, making her feel welcome. Simon had gone to buy her a drink while they waited for their table to be made ready.

"This is nice," she said as they found a cosy corner away from the other guests.

"I thought you'd like it. It's more your style than some of our London haunts. That's Patsy's scene, not yours, yet if you'd let me, I could have taken you to places you'd have liked, Phil. It always amazes me how different you are, you and Patsy. I must have been an idiot not to have seen before that you are the beauty, my dear

Philomena. Patsy can't hold a candle to you."

He was leaning over and whispering, his eyes devouring her as he looked at her in the soft lights. Why hadn't he noticed before how attractive she was?

Phil moved away, frowning a little.

"I thought this was supposed to be a friendly evening out. I don't want all these compliments."

"Well you shouldn't have prettied yourself up so much. It's a signal to any man that you are open for business."

A moment later a young woman came to tell them their table was ready and Phil rose thankfully. She was going to need to keep her wits about her in order to keep Simon Browne at arm's length. She should not have come with him. She should have given him a flat refusal.

She looked at him as they sat opposite one another in the charming dining room while the waitress handed each of them a menu. She had thought she loved him at one time and had spent happy wakeful hours dreaming up a wonderful future for both of them, but now he did not attract her in the least.

She chose a starter of prawn cocktail with roast lamb to follow while Simon ordered wine, then she leaned back in her chair. In spite of Simon's attitude towards her, she found that she was enjoying herself.

"This is Delia's favourite haunt," he said, looking round. "She and Bryden Scott come here regularly. I thought they might have been here tonight, but he has gone to Carlisle."

Phil's appetite began to evaporate a little. So Bryden brought Delia Browne here regularly. She, too, looked around imagining them sitting together at one of the attractive tables and jealousy ate into her soul once more. Well, at least they were not here this evening!

"He has gone to Carlisle on business," she said.

"Pleasure, too, I would think. I heard Delia talking on the telephone, then she rushed in to say she had a date for this evening. She was wearing her best dress, too . . . trying to make herself look like Princess Diana, though she's not the type. *You* would have looked much prettier in that dress, Philomena."

She said nothing. The food was delicious and she managed to eat it though her pleasure in the evening had been spoilt.

If Simon had not come barging into her life again, would Bryden have taken her out to Carlisle? She was sure that he would. But she could not match Delia for looks, and certainly not for clothes. Recently she had bought another pretty gown but she could not afford a beautiful dress in the style worn by the Princess.

"You haven't really made friends with Delia, have you?" Simon asked.

"I'm here to work, remember?" she said, lightly. "Besides, I don't exactly move in your circle, Simon."

"No, you don't," he agreed, and she

flushed. If she was so far beneath the Brownes of Highfield, then he should not be asking her out. He wanted to be amused, as she remembered, and once again her eyes were rather apprehensive as she looked at him. He had promised her an evening out with no strings, but she did not trust him. She was going to have to be careful when he took her home. She had been so confident that she could handle Simon . . . but could she?

"What's wrong?" he asked. "You look at me as thought I were a snake."

"It's nothing," she said, quickly.

"You can come to tea at Highfield on Sunday, then you can get to know the place a little better," he told her, kindly.

"Oh no, I don't think so," she returned, shaking her head.

"That's an honour for you, for God's sake!"

"I'm not unaware of it and thank you for asking me, but I don't think so. Your sister would not like it."

"She can lump it. The parents want me to stay at home and help to run Highfield. They insisted that I came home from London even though I was happy there. Now Father says he is getting old and it's time I settled down. Well, if they want me at home, they'll have to accept *my* friends and not the friends *they* choose for me. I shall expect you on Sunday. Don't dress up. Ride over on Darby. Delia thinks you can't ride and are afraid of horses. She thought that was amusing, you know, but you can show her she's wrong. You ride quite well . . . "

"No, I don't," she said, quickly. "I don't at all. I am nervous of horses. She can laugh her head off if she likes, but I'm still nervous of horses. Old Darby is different."

"All the more reason why you should take credit for going out on Darby then."

"He's a nice quiet old thing."

"So is Bryden Scott. Dull, too. His wife used to be bored to death by him. He spent more time creeping around photographing his squirrels, and badgers and field mice than taking her out. She could have had a night out with him if she had covered herself with branches and crawled through the undergrowth. I used to relieve the boredom for her sometimes, poor old Barbara."

"I don't believe you. She *must* have been happy at Murdo Cragg. It's never boring, and there are always people around, trying to get Bryden's autograph if nothing else. I can't even take the dog for a walk for cars driving up and asking directions, then producing photographs and books to be autographed. They stare at the hills around, saying they've seen it all on television. It can be a nuisance sometimes, but it is never boring."

He looked at her very thoughtfully.

"Don't tell me you've fallen for Bryden Scott. That would be a disaster for you, my pet. For one thing, Delia wants him and always gets what she wants, and for another I don't think he'd even notice you, except to hand you letters to be typed. He lives in a different world from the rest of us. Don't waste your time on him, Phil darling."

Her face was scarlet. He always irritated her and he always knew the most hurtful things to say. Sometimes she liked his bright conversation, but he could turn malicious in an instant.

She pushed away the remains of her peach melba and looked at him, her face very white.

"I don't think I want any more, Simon. I think I would like to go back home now."

"Coffee in the lounge," he said, easily. "We are not finished yet."

"I am."

"Oh, no, you're not. You are not finished until I deliver you back again to Murdo Cragg."

★ ★ ★

Clouds had obscured the moon as Simon conducted Phil back to the car which had been parked in front of the hotel. She stumbled a little and he caught her arm, but a moment later she managed to open the car door and slipped inside. He walked round and slid into the driver's seat, then turned the car towards Keswick.

"I had hoped for beautiful moonlight," he told her, and her heart lurched, then grew heavy. It had been such beautiful moonlight when Bryden Scott brought her home from Sharrow Bay. Had Delia been busy that evening? Had he been hard up for a bit of feminine society?

They drove on in silence until Simon eventually turned along the road which led to Murdo Cragg. Then he stopped the car in the lay-by where Bryden had also stopped.

"Why are we stopping?" she asked.

"Why shouldn't we?"

"Not here," she said, quickly.

He had reached for her and now

he drew back, his eyes narrowing at her tone.

"What's wrong with here? I would have expected you to say not anywhere. Can it be that it has special memories for you? Has dear Bryden been kissing you here in the moonlight?"

She caught her breath in a gasp at his perception and he held her wrist in fingers of steel.

"That's it, isn't it? He's quicker off the mark than I would have imagined, and you are a very attractive little typist for him. All bosses make passes at their typists."

"Leave him alone!" said Phil, sharply, "and take me home, Simon. Thank you for the night out, but I'm sure you'll find better companionship for yourself than . . . than me."

"Not yet," he said, easily. "You've had a damn good night out and you can spare me some of your time." He pulled her into his arms in spite of her protests. "You're growing up, Phil, and you weren't bad before. In fact, you were in love with me, whatever you say. A man can always tell and you were mad for me. Relax and we could have a good time again."

"You promised that if I went out with you, it could be for friendship's sake. No strings. That's what you said. Now you're going back on it."

The last word was smothered as he began to kiss her, and Phil tried hard to break free of him, then remained passive but complete unresponsive.

"There," said Simon, "you soon stopped struggling."

"I had no choice. And I'd like to remind you that this is not such a quiet road as you'd imagine. At least three cars have passed. Some of the drivers might even have been your friends."

"So what does that matter? They know that if I want to take a girl out, I'll also want something in return."

His arm reached out, pulling her close again.

"I want a lot more than this, Phil."

"Well, you're not going to get it,"

she said, alarmed.

"I won't force you tonight, but just think about it for next time."

"There won't *be* any next time!"

"Oh, no? I told you I get bored easily away from London, but you can help a lot with relieving the boredom. It's really great that you're working up here. Have you told Bryden Scott about our previous association? And what about Patsy? Have you told him about Patsy? Your only relative is very unprincipled, Philomena. She did knock into his car, then tried to say it was his fault, and to cash in on it. I kept well out of the way, of course, but I was a witness. I must tell him that some time."

"Oh, be quiet!" she cried, her nerves now on edge. He was trying a bit of very subtle blackmail. Unless she 'amused' him while he was at Highfield, he would be running to Bryden with tales which would show her up in a bad light, and show that she came from a poor background.

But Patsy was very young yet,

thought Phil, and less mature than herself in spite of the fact that they were twins. She would learn, in time, that it did not pay to tell lies. And as for their parents, well, she was proud of both of them. They had done their best for her and Patsy and she had loved them.

In any case, if Bryden was going to marry Delia Browne, it hardly mattered.

"It's no use, Simon," she said, "you can't threaten me. You can take me home now."

"Home? Where's home? Murdo Cragg? I doubt if it will be 'home' much longer, my dear. One of those cars which has just passed us belongs to Bryden Scott. He'll understand very well now that we're the best of friends, you and I. Perhaps you won't have to put up with his kisses now. He's too old for you, Phil."

She felt sick at heart. Was it true that Bryden had seen her in Simon's arms? Would he begin to think of her as a girl not worthy of respect? She loved him and she knew that she would be deeply unhappy if he lost any regard he held for her.

"I don't care who saw us, Simon," she said, quietly, "because *I've* done nothing to make me feel ashamed. I think you ought to take me back to Murdo Cragg now. Maybe it isn't my home, but it's all I have at the moment."

He pulled back from her and straightened his tie, and she could see the angry glitter of his eyes.

"Have it your own way."

He started up the car and they drove in silence to Murdo Cragg. He leaned across her to undo the lock of the car, leaving her to push it open herself. Then suddenly he was laughing again and giving her a kiss.

"You're a lot more fun when you make it hard for me, Phil," he said softly. "The best fish are always the ones that got away, but they get caught eventually. I'm not finished with you yet. Don't bother to ride over on Sunday. I'll come and fetch you."

"I don't want to come."

"But I *want* you to come. Be ready at three."

She scrambled out of the car to run indoors. Mrs Cleland had promised to leave the back door unlocked for her but now Phil's heart sank as she went to open it. It had been locked and bolted from inside. She did not possess her own key. All the doors at Murdo Cragg had huge old-fashioned locks with large black keys, and there was always someone in the house.

Phil looked up at Mrs Cleland's bedroom but it was in darkness, as was the kitchen. The older woman must have gone to bed.

Simon had driven away and now Phil stood out in the yard in the darkness of the night, and began to shiver. Her gown and wrap were light and flimsy, and a breeze had now blown in from the Solway. Looking up she could see black clouds scudding across the sky with occasional breaks in the cloud lit up by the moon.

Could she throw some gravel up at Mrs Cleland's window? Or was it possible for her to slide back the heavy kitchen window? It opened sideways and sometimes Mrs Cleland left the latch undone.

Phil tugged at the window, then suddenly the kitchen window flooded with light and the door flew open. She ran towards it, then faltered a little when she saw Bryden standing there.

"Come in," he said, harshly, and grabbed her arm.

As he rebolted the door and turned to her, she could see that he was furiously angry.

"Why didn't you ring the bell, you silly child? You're frozen. And why did that . . . that rat, Simon, not see you safely indoors before he drove away? Is this the way to treat a young woman?"

"It . . . it doesn't matter," she said, her teeth chattering a little. "Mrs

Cleland said she would leave the door unbolted, and — "

"And I locked it when I came in. I don't like unbolted doors at this time of night. We are not immune from burglars, you know. Why invite them in? Sit down and I shall give you a hot drink with a little rum in it to take the chill out of your bones. You need something like that."

"I don't want it," she protested. "I only want to go to bed."

"Well, you'll drink it nevertheless. What good will you be to me if you take to your bed with a chill? You know very well that we have a lot of work to get through at the moment. If it were not that we were so busy . . . "

He did not finish the sentence. He was making her a hot rum and lemon, but Phil could have finished it for him . . . If we were not so busy, I would send you packing, my dear Philomena. You're not the sort of girl I wish to employ.

She could almost hear him saying it,

and she had a sudden overwhelming desire to try to regain whatever regard he had had for her.

"Drink that," he commanded and she sipped the hot liquid, feeling it coursing through her veins and warming her body, and perhaps even her heart.

"You . . . you saw us, Simon and me . . . at the lay-by," she began, huskily.

He had turned away to tidy the lemon and rum from the kitchen table, but now his body seemed to freeze and he stared at her.

"What do you mean . . . saw you? Do you think I've been spying on you? What were you doing anyway, or need I ask?"

The heat, inspired by her drink and now his words, made her cheeks colour furiously. She tried to speak, but couldn't find the words. Simon had lied to her . . . or perhaps he had not. At any rate, Bryden had *not* seen them, and now she had only aroused his anger and contempt.

"What you do in your free time is

your own affair, Philomena," he said evenly, his voice cold as ice. "However, while you are under my roof, I would like you to see as little as possible of Simon Browne. I don't think he is a . . . a desirable companion for you."

"Not so desirable as Delia," she said, jealously, and again he turned to stare at her.

"Certainly Delia Browne is a more worthwhile person than her brother. He was badly spoiled as a boy and it has not made him the sort of man I can respect."

But he could respect Delia. Did he love her? Of course he must love her if he wanted to marry her one day. Why did they wait? she wondered. No doubt it was because Delia felt she could not leave her parents at this time. The pace of life was slower here than in London. There would be plenty of time to arrange a marriage when they were ready, and meantime they could see each other every day and enjoy one another's company. The thought made her jealousy rise again.

"Thank you for your concern," she said, her voice still husky, "but I've promised to go with Simon to Highfield for tea on Sunday. Three o'clock."

Her tone was defiant and he came to look closely into her face.

"Tea on Sunday, three o'clock," he repeated.

"He . . . he wants to show me Highfield. I don't know the place at all well."

"It's a fine property. You could do worse, Philomena, except that Simon Browne goes with that property and he doesn't always have marriage in mind. There's a snag in everything, isn't there? I said to be careful and I mean it."

She finished her hot drink, then she stood up, very much aware of him, though he did not touch her, not even to put a hand on her arm.

"If he kissed you goodnight, then I shall not follow his lead, Philomena," Bryden said quietly. "I will never touch a girl who has only just left the arms of Simon Browne."

"You must hate him a great deal," she said, wonderingly. "You . . . You make me feel as though I . . . I were contaminated."

"I'm sorry, my dear, of course I don't think that about you. Though you could be, if you make him your closest companion. Yes, that's how I feel about Simon."

Yet he was willing to have him for a brother-in-law!

"I might go with you to Highfield on Sunday," he said, reflectively. "Was he coming to collect you, did you say? You can telephone and say that I shall bring you. I have a standing invitation to Highfield on Sundays."

He was using his employer's tone and automatically she nodded.

"Very well, if you think that will be acceptable to Miss Browne."

"It will be acceptable."

She turned away and he touched her arm.

"Goodnight, Philomena."

Suddenly his tone was kind again and the kindness was her undoing. She could not explain why she wanted to cry her eyes out, but she did. Picking up her wrap, she climbed the stairs to her bedroom.

8

BRYDEN'S book made slow but steady progress and he took many photographs and worked hard at illustrations. But his agent in London was still uncertain about the television series, and Bryden tried to shrug off any anxiety.

Phil had come to know him rather better and she could see that he would be very disappointed if his new ideas were not acceptable. It was easy to lose touch with the people who enjoyed his programmes. If he could not supply material for a new, different type of programme, he might lose a great deal of what he had worked for over the years. Already fewer people were calling to see the background of his earlier work, and it was generally known that his small, delightful squirrel family had all gone.

"They were the real stars," he said sadly to Phil one day. "I loved them. They were delightful pets, especially Betsy. Her bright eyes were so full of charm."

"But someone killed her," said Phil.

Bryden's voice was harsh. "Yes, someone killed her."

There was silence, and Phil felt there was nothing she could say.

"And the other two?" she asked at length.

"They sickened and I could not save them. Since then I have brought up a baby kestrel and the baby owl, but neither became part of the household like Betsy though I tried to keep their natural habitat as far as possible. The birds had to be returned to the wild. Betsy refused to leave home. She delighted us with her beauty and charm. Ah well, it is all in the past. We mustn't be tempted to live in the past, Philomena. You understand?"

She thought about Simon Browne and how he was always raking up her past and using it against her.

"Not even if . . . if it makes one feel ashamed?" she asked.

He had been about to leave the study, but now he came to stand beside her.

"What have you done to make you feel ashamed?"

"I didn't say it was me!"

"No, but it isn't hard to guess."

"I didn't mean anything by it," she said, shaking her head almost wildly. "I was only speaking in generalities."

She could not confess that she had once allowed Simon to take hold of her heart. Yet it had been a short-lived attraction. She had recovered from it very soon. But now she wished it had never happened, and especially she wished that Patsy had never tried to play tricks on Bryden Scott. He was a man of such high integrity. He must have despised Patsy, having seen through her wiles. And Patsy was her twin sister.

She raised tormented eyes to him.

151

"You knew Simon Browne in the past?" he asked.

She nodded slowly.

"I meant what I said, Philomena," he told her. "Simon is not welcome in my home."

He got up and strolled around the room, then he heaved a great sigh.

"Why am I behaving like this?" he asked. "I've just told you that we mustn't live in the past, yet that's exactly what I am doing. I bear Simon a grudge from the past, yet it is all over now. He is older, for one thing. He was only a silly boy then. And why should I punish you for something which is not your fault? No, if you wish to entertain Simon here, you may do so. I've been wrong to forbid it. I tend to forget how young you are, and that you need the companionship of young people. The years pile on, and a man is no longer young. One forgets."

"But *you* are young!" cried Phil. "You are a young man, not old."

He smiled rather sadly. "I am a

great deal older than you, Philomena. Nevertheless I have rung up Highfield and I will take you over on Sunday. We will go together."

She felt relieved and her heart lightened at the prospect. If she were honest with herself, she knew that she had no wish to go to Highfield. It was Simon's home, and Delia's, and she wanted nothing to do with either of them. Delia Browne made her feel very much aware of the fact that she was a girl of very little importance to anyone, and if Simon wished to entertain her in his own home, she knew that Delia would not be ready to make her feel welcome.

Would it be any better if she went with Bryden? If Delia was inclined to be withering to Bryden's secretary, he might show his disapproval, and in addition, Simon would not be able to manoeuvre her into an embarrassing situation if Bryden was keeping an eye on her. Was he also aware of this? she wondered. Was that why he was taking her, or was it because he merely wanted to be with Delia? Perhaps he took every opportunity available to do just that. He rarely did things without a purpose behind them.

Again Phil was beset by jealousy. She longed for a fairy godmother who would wave a magic wand and make Bryden forget about Delia Browne, and fall in love with her. Nothing that had gone before would matter a bit, and Bryden would not keep noticing that she was only a young girl. The fairy godmother would give her maturity, and all would be well.

So went Phil's dreams as she typed out Bryden's notes and answered the telephone. She never used to daydream quite so much, except when she fancied herself in love with Simon. Now she did it all the time.

★ ★ ★

Highfield was an opulent house and might have been designed to make Phil feel over-awed, but she found the soft cushions and ornate furniture of the Victorian era rather suffocating, and longed to open the big windows which were curtained in heavy plush. She had an overall impression of maroon and gold with dark rugs on a plain beige carpet.

Delia came to meet them, with Simon following behind her, looking sulky. There was an angry sparkle in Delia's eyes and Phil wondered if they'd had a row.

"How good of you to come with Miss . . . ah . . . Philomena," said Delia, greeting Bryden with a warm kiss on the cheek. She touched Phil's fingers lightly and accepted the box of chocolates she had brought with surprised laughter.

"But how kind! What a pity I don't eat chocolates, but they are so useful to offer to guests."

"Hello, Phil," said Simon. "You, too, Scott. I asked Phil over so that I could show her Highfield, but we seem to have made a tea party of it. I hate tea, so I won't be having any, but I can fix my own drink."

"I doubt if there will be much at Highfield to interest a city girl," said Delia. "We are old-fashioned here," she said, complacently. "Our roots go deep."

"Only as far back as Grandfather," said Simon.

"That's quite far. I doubt if Philomena even remembers *her* grandfather. But there were Scotts at Murdo Cragg as far back as the sixteenth century. That's so, isn't it, Bryden?"

"You're the one who likes to look up old church records," he said, lightly. "I hear you are now secretary to the parochial church council, Delia."

"Only while Mother is away. She has been secretary for years."

Phil accepted a cup of lukewarm Lapsang-Souchong in a shallow Crown Derby cup, and a tiny ham sandwich. Delia had positioned herself behind the silver teapot at a small table set for four in the drawing room. She wore an elegant seagreen silk dress and her beauty and composure made Phil feel small and insignificant by comparison. Yet there was a shabbiness to the grandeur at Highfield which gradually became apparent to Phil. It was as though time had moved on and left Highfield to slip very gradually into decay. Murdo Cragg was a rambling old house, but the rooms were bright and comfortable. Even the study, which was a man's room through and through, had an air of permanence and comfort. Phil did not feel comfortable at Highfield.

After the first few words of greeting, Delia decided to ignore Phil and to address herself almost exclusively to Bryden. The Meet had been postponed, and now this was to be held in another week.

"You *will* come, won't you, darling?" she asked. "I'm arranging refreshments here at Highfield, and Simon can take Father's place. The parents have decided to stay on for another month."

"We will try to come," Bryden nodded, "though no promises, Delia, since we are at a difficult part of the book. But it might be an experience for Philomena."

"From what she has said, it is hardly one she is likely to enjoy," said Delia, sharply, "and I don't think Darby a very suitable mount for riding to hounds."

"I would not like to ride out chasing foxes," said Phil.

"Ride to hounds," Delia repeated with satisfaction. "I thought you would not."

"She can still come," said Simon. "I insist on it. She can stay here and help with the refreshments . . . entertaining our guests and all that."

"I do not wish to come," said Phil, glancing at Bryden with heightened colour in her cheeks. "I don't like hunting."

"She's a city girl," Delia repeated.

"What's that got to do with it? I've

told you you needn't *hunt*, Phil," said Simon with irritation. "I want you to come."

"She need not, if she does not wish to be here," said Bryden. "She can make up her own mind."

Phil thought that everyone was making her mind up for her, except herself! Certainly Delia did not want her at Highfield, and Simon was now scowling and in a very bad mood because things were not going according to how he wished.

Once or twice he had offered to take her round the place on her own since Bryden had no need to come, but always Delia had found some excuse. The last time, he had been sent for more hot water and a cloth to wipe up a little spot of cream she had spilled on the lacy tablecloth.

"Use a napkin," he had said, but Delia thought that a damp cloth would be better.

Phil wished herself back at Murdo Cragg. This visit was proving a disaster.

At times like these she realised how happy she was as she worked her way through a normal day, but at times like these, she also realised that she could not stay at Murdo Cragg for ever. Things were bound to change one day, with no benefit to herself.

She jerked herself out of her thoughts as she realised that the others were looking at her again. They had finished tea and an elderly maidservant had cleared everything away. Now Phil's cheeks coloured a little. She would have to stop worrying and day-dreaming like this.

"I . . . I'm sorry," she apologised. "Did you say something . . . ?"

"I only asked if you would be kind enough to play for us," said Bryden, rather coolly. She could see a glint in his eye which warned her to pay a little more attention.

Phil was at a loss how to reply. She glanced around and saw a large grand piano standing in the corner of the room.

"The piano is my mother's," said Delia. "She loathes pop music."

"Philomena does not play pop music," said Bryden.

"So she has been playing for you? On Barbara's piano?"

He flushed. "I'm sure that Barbara would have been the last to object."

His eyes had turned to Simon who retreated a little.

"You all live in the past," he said. "You're always chewing it over."

"Perhaps it is a bad thing to dwell too much in the past," Delia agreed, "though I don't know what it has to do with . . . with this girl."

"I only asked if you would like Philomena to play for us," said Bryden with a certain edge to his tone so that Delia almost immediately climbed down and turned to Phil with a smile which was rather too bright.

"But of *course* she must play for us, if she does not mind. But today she is our guest. Bryden, dear, one does not invite a guest to tea, then ask her to work. However, I should be delighted so long as she understands this."

She spoke to Bryden, then looked enquiringly at Phil who wished she was elsewhere at that moment. What was Bryden Scott thinking about? He must see that he was putting her in an embarrassing position.

Obediently, however, she rose to her feet and went over to the piano. It was not in quite such good condition as the one at Murdo Cragg and she ran her fingers over it, striking one or two notes which were out of tune.

"It needs tuning, I know," said Delia with a light laugh. "That will be a good excuse if you are out of practice, Miss Blake."

What should she play? Phil wondered nervously. If it were one of the light bubbly pieces her father had loved, it would no doubt be amusing to Delia Browne, who would consider it simple and sentimental. On the other hand, if she tried to play something ambitious, wouldn't that make it appear that she wished to impress her hosts with her playing?

Then almost without thinking her fingers were rippling over the keys in one of her own favourites, 'The First Rustle of Spring', followed by Mendelssohn's 'Song without words'. The piano was stiff with lack of use, but Phil managed to coax the keys into some form of discipline, and the music filled the large opulent room with its own beauty.

Simon had come to stand beside her and would have begun to sort through his mother's music, proud that Phil could play so well in front of his sister, if she had not stopped him.

"I don't wish to bore the audience," she said in a low voice.

"Well, what did you bring Scott for?" he hissed. "I would have come for you myself. I wanted to show you the garden. We have a super summer-house. It's a bit broken down but nobody ever goes there. I would soon have got rid of Delia."

"I'm glad you can't show it to me," she said, in an equally low voice. "I don't like your suggestions, Simon. There's no future in trying to amuse yourself at my expense."

"Oh, no? You think I don't hold any cards? Is that it? You can wriggle out of the one I do hold. Well, I haven't used some of them yet. I've got a few tricks up my sleeve."

"I'm sure you have," she said, sweetly. "I don't play cards, myself. I hate such games. I think you'd better put that music away, Simon. I really have played enough for one day."

Delia was showing Bryden Scott the postcards she had received from her parents when Phil came over to join them once more.

"Finished your little pieces?" asked Delia, brightly.

Her tone was so patronising that Phil caught her lip between her teeth. She had not wanted to play at all. She hated playing one or two short 'pieces' in a situation like this. Either she put on a full programme with Patsy, or she did not play at all, except for keeping in practice. She was even more hurt when Bryden looked up from studying the postcards and looked with obvious amusement from herself to Delia.

"I'm glad you enjoyed it, Delia," he said, lightly. "I could envy your parents this moment. I would enjoy a holiday in the sun. However . . . "

He looked around, then picked up Phil's purse, pushing it into her hands. "Time to go. Nice of you to invite us, Delia."

He bent and kissed her cheek.

"Don't forget the Meet, darling," she insisted.

"We'll do our best to be present."

Phil firmed her lips, knowing that Bryden was still going to do his best to see that she was present. Why was he doing this? she wondered. Could it be that he was not yet ready to marry Delia, and was using her as some sort of chaperone? Did he, perhaps, now feel that his finances were not sound enough for marriage? Or could it be that *he* was the chaperone, intent on keeping her away from Simon? He had certainly ensured that they were not alone. Would he do the same at the Meet?

Phil had never been so pleased to be out into the fresh air once more. She found the interior of Highfield overpowering which might not have mattered had she felt welcome in Delia Browne's home. But the older girl did not try to hide her disapproval of Phil. And yet it was hardly even disapproval. Delia found her so insignificant that it was an irritation to her when she was forced to acknowledge Phil's existence. She probably knew that Simon had cultivated a number of 'little friends' in London and thought that Phil was one of them. Now Delia's eyes sparkled with anger every time Bryden Scott was at all deferential to the girl.

Bryden was even now opening the car door and settling her inside, and she breathed a sigh of relief as they drove along the gravelled drive with laurels and rhododendrons on either side, very similar to Murdo Cragg. Phil's shoulder still smarted where the pressure of Simon's fingers had dug into her.

"Don't think I'm finished with you," he had whispered in her ear. "I'm only beginning. In fact, you are making this a lot of fun, Phil. I quite like being back home."

"Leave me alone, Simon," she had pleaded. "I've got a job to do. Just . . . just let me get on with it."

"Not when Bryden Scott tries to spoil my fun," he had said. "I know what's in his mind. He treated me like something which had crawled from under a stone."

"When? What for?"

"Never you mind. All in the past, but he won't do it again. So remember, I'll be calling for you and I want no arguments. I'll get tickets for a dinner dance at The Castle. We'll go to that together."

She had been shaking her head when Bryden took her arm and guided her towards the car. They drove home in silence, but Phil hardly noticed. The moon was full, throwing weird ghostly light over the countryside and the shadows of tall trees fell into the road in front of the car, making it seem almost as bright as daylight. Phil had never known that moonlight could look so beautiful, and she leaned forward in the car as Bryden braked suddenly to allow a small woodland creature to run towards the safety of the hedge.

When they arrived back at Murdo Cragg, he sat still for a moment then turned to Phil. In the brightness of the light, she could see his black eyes glittering, and her heart beat with excitement and anticipation. He was going to kiss her, thought Phil, and she did not care whether or not he was going to marry Delia Browne one day. She did not care about anything other than this wild fierce love she felt for him. She knew he would never marry her, but she would settle for what he had to offer, at least for now. At first her pride had been uppermost, but now she would forego that pride. She only wanted a little part of Bryden's love.

But he made no movement towards her. Instead he laid a hand on her arm.

"I have taken you to Highfield," he said, quietly, "and protected you when Simon Browne might have placed you in a difficult position. I know very well what is in his mind, you know. I have tried to give you some pride in yourself, and in your own accomplishments. Now I expect you to behave with dignity and to have a proper respect for Philomena Blake. I can't prevent you from accepting invitations from Browne, but I must ask you to think carefully before you become involved with him. He's not a fit companion for a young woman like you. I . . . " He turned away and opened the car door at his side. "I wish I did not feel so responsible for you. I wish you had

169

some relative I could approach."

His voice faded and stopped as he walked round to her side of the car and opened the door. Phil's legs felt like cottonwool as she stepped out and stood beside him. She felt deeply humiliated. She had thought he might find her attractive and would want to kiss her. Instead he was treating her like a very young girl who needed his protection. He did not see her as a woman at all, or if he did, she was no longer attractive to him after Delia.

"Goodnight, Philomena," he said, courteously.

She drew a deep breath and managed to force back the tears which were gathering at the back of her throat.

"Goodnight, Bryden. Thank you for taking me."

9

PHIL worked very hard over the next week or two and when her typing was finished, she tidied up papers, old bills, business accounts and general paperwork, polishing the cabinets and desks until Bryden ordered her to take time off for relaxation.

"You'll wear yourself to a shadow," he told her, but she made no reply. It was better to work hard, otherwise she felt miserable and depressed. She would have to return to London soon, and try to begin a new life. Bryden might guess how she felt about him, and Phil could not bear to watch his embarrassment and his kindness. She preferred him to be irritable and to ask her to re-type a page if he found a mistake.

Simon telephoned several times, but she managed to put him off. She had no wish to spend any time with Simon and a small spark of hope was gradually re-born in her heart. Why was Bryden so much against her seeing Simon? Could it be that he was just a little jealous? He must care about her a little, or he would not go to such trouble over her. If he did not care about her, surely he would not mind whether she was seeing Simon, or not.

The faint hope took root in her heart and happiness began to flow once more. For daily exercise she still rode Darby, but occasionally she took the small pony and trap out on the quiet roads over the moors. She found she could handle the pony and trap better than the horse and she began to look forward to having an hour off by herself and driving up into the fells to eat the picnic lunch which Mrs Cleland prepared for her.

She was about to pack away her lunch-box one day and to return the book she was reading to her briefcase when a car drove along the lonely moorland road and minutes later it drew up beside her and Simon climbed out.

"So *this* is where you are!" he said accusingly. "That Cleland woman needs to pack her bags. She was positively rude to me. She would only say that you had gone out and there was no hint at all about where you had gone, or when you would be back."

Phil rose to her feet, then backed away. At the back of her mind she had known that she would see Simon again one of these days, and she was unsure what to say to him. It was one thing for Bryden to tell her to avoid Simon Browne, but quite another to carry out his wishes!

"I was just going, Simon," she said, hurriedly. "I only have an hour or so off in the mornings or afternoons to get some fresh air, then I have to be back to get on with more work. I'm afraid I've got to go now."

He stared at her suspiciously.

"You're avoiding me! That's it, isn't it? You keep putting me off. You know we got on very well at one time. Okay, I made a mistake. I thought I wanted Patsy rather than you, but that's all changed now, Phil. I really meant it when I told you that. In fact, I think I'm in love with you. I'm even enough in love with you to want to marry you, and that's why I wanted you to come over to Highfield and to get to know my sister before the parents get back. She's not such a bad sort when you get to know Delia. It's a pity she's such a horsey woman, and you're not, but if you come to the Meet and look pretty, and hand round the sherry and biscuits, she'll see that you will do okay. Bryden Scott will bring you. We can tell him we're engaged, though better not make it public till the parents get back."

"No!" cried Phil. "No . . . please, Simon . . . "

She was trying to stop him. He had come over to pull her into his arms and now she was backing away so that his face began to redden and his eyes narrowed.

"I don't think you quite understand, Philomena," he said, clearly. "I've told you, I'll go all the way. Marriage. No girl has ever got that much out of me before. That's how much I care about you. I don't suppose the parents will be best pleased at first, but we'll soon wear them down."

"I *do* appreciate it!" she cried, "but . . . but I . . . "

Suddenly there was a sound behind them and two riders hove into view. Phil's heart bounded, then sank as she saw that it was Bryden and Delia, and that the hard harsh look was back on his face when he saw that she was with Simon. He and Delia had dismounted and were walking towards them.

"So *this* is where you are," said Bryden coldly. "I expect you to let Donald Douglas know where you are going when you come out on the fells, Philomena, in case of accidents. This pony and trap are not so easy for an inexperienced young woman to manage.

"I find them easier than Darby," said Phil, though the warmth had surged into her cheeks when she saw the look on his face. It was clear that he thought she had arranged to meet Simon at this spot, and had deliberately flouted his wishes. Yet what right had he to dictate to her about her friends? she thought, indignantly. He liked going out with his own friends. Suppose someone tried to stop him from seeing Delia! She could imagine what sort of reception they would receive. If only she liked Simon better, she would certainly leave Bryden in no doubt that she was still her own mistress, even if she were very dependent on him at the moment.

"Dearie me, such a fuss!" Delia was saying as she sauntered forward. "We've been combing the countryside for your poor broken body, Philomena, and the crashed remains of the trap with the pony half way to Ravenglass.

Now we find you keeping dates with Simon. I should have remembered that he likes quiet spots like this."

"Now mind what you say, Delia," put in Simon, quickly. "This is different. Phil and I are engaged, but you'd better not make it public until the parents get home."

"Oh, no!" cried Phil.

"It's okay, I can tell Delia, darling. She's got to know."

"But I haven't . . . I mean, we aren't . . . "

Her eyes flew to Bryden's. His face had gone very white and hard. He looked as though he were furiously angry and her voice faltered as she stared at him.

"Well, I'm not sure whether or not congratulations are in order," Delia was saying. "As you say, Simon, you'd better wait until the parents get home. I think Father will want to have some sort of say in your choice of bride. After all, you are completely dependent on him, are you not?"

Simon flushed. "He can't run my life for me."

"Perhaps not, but he can make it uncomfortable. Your new fiancée had better know how you stand financially in case she thinks her money troubles are over."

Angry tears rushed to Phil's eyes.

"How *dare* you say such a thing!" she cried. "I would *never* marry for such a reason."

"Since you are so capable of managing your own affairs, including the pony and trap, I shall see you back at the house as soon as it is convenient," said Bryden so harshly that all three were startled. He had swung himself back in the saddle, and now he nodded to Delia, then pulled away. A moment later he had gone.

"Oh dear, I forgot that Bryden does not like to discuss finances in public. And he's no doubt feeling guilty because he brought you here, Philomena, and now we might be landed with a heap of trouble."

"Not if you help, Delia," Simon was saying. "I mean, this time I'm in love. I really want Phil, and I must have her. You'll help, won't you?"

But Phil had had enough. Already she was climbing into the trap.

"We are not engaged," she said, clearly, to Simon. "There is no need for all this talk. I am not going to marry you."

Delia Browne was leaning against Simon's car.

"Oh, I wouldn't give up so easily, my dear," she said, casually. "As a matter of fact, I thought you were trying to get your little claws into Bryden. I'm rather pleased that it was Simon all the time. Bryden isn't for you. But you don't really play the piano too badly. We could put you over as a concert pianist. After all they had to put up with Simon's crazy friends from London. They might be pleased enough if he settled down with a concert pianist."

Phil did not want to argue any more, but Simon had come to stand up in

179

the trap, and now he leaned over and kissed her.

"I'll see you soon, Phil darling," he promised. "You see? Delia isn't so bad when you take her the right way."

"*No* Simon!" she cried. "I told you . . . no!"

"Don't be frightened. Even Father is not such an ogre when he's got used to an idea, and you could soon get round him. You're pretty enough, and just between ourselves, he likes a pretty face."

Phil's head was now aching badly. She could hardly believe that she was slowly getting herself into a mess through no fault of her own. Simon Browne had been so spoilt all his life that he had never needed to take 'no' for an answer. He had always got what he wanted. Now he wanted her. How could she make him understand that she did not want him?

And how could she make Bryden understand that she had no interest in Simon and was certainly not going to marry him? He could be so unapproachable when something angered or displeased him, and never before had she seen him looking at her as he had done a short time ago.

"Very touching," Delia was saying, "but if Phil is moving off, I shall ride quietly behind her and see that she *does* get back to Murdo Cragg. I don't want another session with Bryden. I've more to do than go chasing off after lost girls, even if you're going to be my sister-in-law. Don't worry, Philomena, we'll sort our Mother and Father."

But Phil was already on her way though her nerves and anger seemed to communicate itself to the pony and she knew she was not handling him at all well on her journey home. Delia knew it, too.

"I shall tell Bryden to forbid you to go out with the pony and trap," she said when they reached Murdo Cragg. "You're a positive danger to yourself, *and* to everyone else. You'll have to do better than that if you're going to live at Highfield one day."

Phil made no reply. Gratefully she allowed Donald Douglas to help her out of the trap, then she practically staggered indoors and burst into tears in Mrs Cleland's arms.

"Did that beastie run away with you, Miss Phil?" she asked in sympathy. "I don't like them horses myself. Never did. They're too lumbering for me. And Mr Bryden was in such a tizzy with himself. He had a phone call, you know. I couldn't help hearing. I think it was about the television and it upset and displeased him. That was when he wanted you and Donald Douglas said you were out with the pony and trap, and had not come back. So off he went to find you. He's back again, but I've never seen such glowering looks since he was once upset over Mrs Barbara. When she and poor little Lee were killed, he was quite different. He went all quiet with his grief, but he came to terms with it in the long run. This time, though, he's angry. I'd keep out of his way for a wee while, Miss Phil."

"He may want me for work," she said.

"Well, he'll soon let you know. Sit down and I'll pour you a good strong cup of tea. Did the beastie tumble you?"

"No. It . . . it was something else," she said, running a hand through her hair as she sat at the kitchen table.

"Well, say no more till you've had your tea," Mrs Cleland said with ready sympathy. "You look as though you need it. Did you hurt yourself, Miss Philomena?"

She looked at Mrs Cleland, biting her lip, then she decided she'd have to confide in someone.

"I got involved in a misunderstanding, that's all," she said, rather wearily. "Mr Bryden thinks I've promised to marry Mr Simon Browne, but . . . "

"Oh dear," cried Mrs Cleland, "that would upset him! That would stir up old wounds."

Phil stared. "What do you mean, Mrs Cleland?"

The older woman turned away and busied herself among her pots and pans.

"I don't like gossip in the kitchen and I always said I would never do it, but I don't like to see Mr Bryden hurt either, and you can hurt him a lot through ignorance. Maybe I'm the only person who knows, too. I don't think Miss Browne or Mr Simon realised the whole of it."

"Of what, Mrs Cleland?"

Phil suddenly experienced a curious shiver of apprehension at the woman's tone.

"Of what happened to Mrs Barbara and . . . and the baby. You see, Mrs Barbara was a very bonny lady, as you can see from her picture. Just like a wild poppy, as Mr Bryden used to say. He doted on her, you see. But she wasn't used to the quiet life of Murdo Cragg. Not that it's so quiet, but she liked the theatres and dinner dances and dressing herself in fancy clothes. And, of course, Mr Bryden was kept busy with his writing and looking after the squirrels. I don't think he saw that she was unsettled in any way."

Mrs Cleland came to sit at the kitchen table.

"And the wee one was such a quiet child. No bother. You never heard her in the house. In fact, I always thought her a bit *too* quiet, and I think Mrs Barbara was concerned about her so that she had things on her mind.

"Then Mr Simon started coming over from Highfield. He had just left the university and some said he left without his degree for some reason. At any rate, he started taking Mrs Barbara out. She wasn't so much older than he was. Only one night they went out together for a long time and the wee baby got sickly. I had to get the doctor, and dear knows what he told Mr Bryden, but it upset him a lot. Next day he and Mrs Barbara had a terrible row, and it was only a day or two after that when she took off with the baby, and crashed her car. Mr Bryden took it very hard. He didn't blame Mr Simon for it all, of course, but I think he felt that the young man had not helped. He unsettled Mrs Barbara. She wasn't the same woman after he came, always looking for entertainment and excitement . . . saying the place was dull. It's not at all dull, Miss Philomena, not if you can enjoy the life it offers."

"No, it isn't dull," said Phil, automatically, though her thoughts were elsewhere. No wonder Bryden did not care for Simon Browne and had asked her not to see him. Yet the cases were not parallel. Barbara had been his wife, whilst she was only a temporary secretarial assistant. It was not as though he cared about her in that way. He had only kissed her once, as many men kissed a girl they had taken out for the evening.

But Simon must have known that he was not welcome at Murdo Cragg.

And what about Delia Browne? Did she know that Simon had been seeing Barbara Scott? Was that why Simon had gone to London to live? Phil's thoughts buzzed round in her head as she drank the cup of strong tea which Mrs Cleland had placed in front of her.

"I'm telling you this so that you'll maybe be able to understand Mr Bryden a little better," the housekeeper said, gently. "He might seem harsh with you, but he has his reasons."

"But he must be getting over it, if he's going to marry Delia Browne," Phil said.

Mrs Cleland's lips firmed.

"I don't know anything about that. *He* has never mentioned such a thing to me. No, I think he still clings to his memory of Mrs Barbara. He took that *very* ill. I don't see that he's over that yet, and whereas he is friendly enough with Miss Delia and is very neighbourly, I don't know that he's ready to put her in Mrs Barbara's place. Mind you, there's a likeness between those two ladies, both being so dark, but Mrs Barbara was outstanding in looks. When she was dressed up, I never saw a bonnier lady. Though, of course, you are bonny yourself, Miss Philomena when you get yourself dressed up. I thought so last time I saw you, but . . . "

"But I can't compete with the wild poppy," said Phil, though her heart ached for Bryden Scott all over again. How he must have been hurt by his wife's death.

"I don't think there's any need for competition," said Mrs Cleland. "The poor lady is dead now, and the wee one besides. It was a great tragedy in Mr Bryden's life and I never thought to see him getting over it. But this past few weeks I've heard him whistling again as he went about his business, and that's a good sign. He was always whistling and cheerful in the old days. But, of course, it's bound to come over him again at times, especially since Mr Simon

Browne has come home again. That young man seems to get Mr Bryden's temper up. That's why he won't want him near Murdo Cragg, and you'll see that it isn't easy for you either, Miss Philomena, if you're going to marry Mr Browne. Highfield is a close neighbour. There are always comings and goings, and when Colonel and Mrs Browne come home from abroad, there will be other invitations. People live close to one another here, even if it appears that your nearest neighbour is a few miles away."

"I'm not going to marry Simon, Mrs Cleland."

"Well, of course, that's nothing to do with me. I just thought I'd tell you, Miss Philomena, then you would know."

"I appreciate it," said Phil.

"Will you be wanting anything else?"

Now that she had confided the family gossip to Phil, Mrs Cleland was quiet and rather huffy. She felt uneasy and ashamed that she had broken her rule and let out family secrets, but at the same time, she did not like to see the girl being influenced by the Brownes from Highfield. That young Simon was not a dependable man in her opinion. Miss Phil could surely do better than him.

10

WHEN Philomena finally went down to the study and nervously pushed open the door, Bryden was talking on the telephone. The anger had gone from his face, but as he turned to look at her, she saw that the special warmth which was always in his eyes when they talked together, had also gone. He was completely impersonal. He waved a hand at a bundle of letters with notes pinned to them, and she picked them up and carried them to her desk.

She paid little attention to the telephone call which appeared to be a personal one, then as Bryden hung up the receiver, she turned to him, determined to clear the air and set things straight with regard to Simon.

"Bryden, with regard to Simon Browne," she began, "I am — "

"Nothing to discuss," he interrupted brusquely. "That was Heather . . . Heather Grant. Her mother is a great deal better, and she would like to come back on Monday week."

It was like a body blow and Phil felt almost physically sick. She had less than a fortnight left to her at Murdo Cragg. After that she would have to return to London and begin the gruelling search for work, and some sort of accommodation.

"I see," she said, quietly.

He was staring at her, then he sighed.

"Perhaps it is better this way, Philomena. We will talk things over at a later date and decide what is best to be done. For the moment we must get down to finishing the last chapter of the book. I've made alterations here and there, and I want you to type it exactly as I have laid it out. I have to leave for London tomorrow and I would like to take this with me. Can you manage those few more pages?"

"Certainly, sir."

He frowned. "No need for that."

"Sorry . . . Bryden."

Again he looked at her uneasily, then he began to say something but changed his mind.

"All right. Well, I shall leave you to it. I have a few other arrangements to make before tomorrow."

Phil was glad to have work to do in order to keep herself from thinking. Her typing had improved enormously and she completed the last few pages of the text of the book in record time, setting out the manuscript with its copy neatly on the desk. Then she turned her attention to the letters, but there were too many of them for one day's work and she was tired when Bryden finally came to tell her that she had done all that was required of her for one day. He was going out for the evening and Phil's thoughts went immediately to Delia Browne. It seemed to her that Mrs Cleland was wrong about one thing. Bryden's friendship with Delia was a great deal closer than the housekeeper knew.

It was difficult to avoid Simon after Bryden had gone. He arrived shortly afterwards in his car and invited Phil back to Highfield to help with preparations for the Meet on Saturday.

"Scott won't mind," he said. "It will be good experience for you to see how things are done."

"I have letters to do, Simon," she said, firmly, "and I don't want to know about Saturday. I am not coming, and that is final."

"Oh, but you've *got* to come," he insisted. "I want you to be there."

Phil closed her eyes for a moment, then she drew a deep breath.

"Please, Simon," she said, very quietly. "Please understand. We are *not* engaged to be married . . . "

"Not yet, but that's why I'm here. You need a ring. There is a family ring, of course, but I would like you to have one of your own. We can go into Carlisle this afternoon."

Suddenly her heart was touched by

his persistence. At least *someone* cared about her, and wanted her, and Simon cared enough about her to buy her a ring. Besides, in another two weeks she would be homeless, and a great many girls would jump at the chance of marrying Simon Browne of Highfield, as he so often told her. Now she knew that this was quite true.

For a long moment she was tempted. It would mean a secure future and she had cared about Simon at one time. Then she put temptation behind her. She did not love Simon. In spite of everything, she loved Bryden Scott, even if he would no doubt have difficulty in remembering her name in another month or so.

"No, Simon," she said, gently. "I don't love you. I can't marry you. I'm sorry."

He paused and looked at her incredulously.

"You really mean that, don't you? You aren't just being coy. You! A mere nobody! And you're turning me down.

I don't believe this. I've had all the girls I want, and I haven't proposed to *one* of them, except you. And you turn me down! You just don't understand. Any *one* of my girls . . . I only had to lift a finger . . . "

"Including Barbara Scott," she said.

He stared. "So he's been talking to you."

She could have bitten her tongue out. "He hasn't said a word."

"Then it's that old harridan. What does she know? Barbara was bored, that's all. I did her a favour. There was nothing in it."

Didn't he know that Bryden and Barbara Scott had quarrelled over him? Didn't he realise what he had done?

"Don't think I am pleading with you," he was saying. "I don't have to go down on my knees to any girl. Okay, so you want to end up in some old dump playing the piano for a few gins . . . "

"Don't!" whispered Phil.

"Or do you think you might be clever

enough to land your fish? Bryden Scott? I'll tell you something, Philomena. You might think he's a big name with his books and television, but that's nothing to the big name he is around here. The Scotts and his mother's people, the Brydens, have been here for hundreds of years. They used to own a huge estate further north, but it burned to the ground at the turn of the century. They were left with their hunting lodge, Murdo Cragg, and their name. Some people might even say my sister was not good enough for him."

"That's just silly!" she cried. "In this day and age? I don't believe all this."

It would be true with regard to herself, but hardly with regard to Delia Browne.

"You'll see. Don't think that if you turn me down, you might get him, because you won't."

How unpleasant he could look when he was angry, she thought, but now she no longer cared. She only had two weeks left here, and for a moment the picture Simon painted of her future made her feel sick.

Then her courage returned. Why should it be that way? If she clung to her own integrity, she could surely take care of herself better than that.

"I'm sorry, Simon," she said, quietly, and he turned and rushed from the room. Reaction set in, and a few minutes later, Phil was in tears. The door opened gently and Mrs Cleland put a tray of coffee and biscuits beside her on the desk. As quietly she slipped out again and Phil drank the coffee gratefully. Then she set about clearing the work she was doing prior to the return of Miss Heather Grant.

* * *

Bryden returned a day or two later, looking quiet and rather grave.

"You might as well know, Philomena," he told her, "that there will be no television series. Disappointing, but there it is."

She hardly knew what to say. He had put such a lot into the planning of a possible programme and she knew how much he loved portraying his own particular brand of wildlife to younger viewers.

"And the book?" she asked.

"Oh, that's okay. But I would like to talk over one or two other ideas with you."

"With Miss Grant," she put in swiftly. "Don't forget that she's coming back in another week."

"Oh, yes." He rumpled his hair. "I had not forgotten."

Next morning the post brought a letter to Phil from Patsy in New York, and she carried it up to her bedroom so that she could read it quietly by herself. Patsy's engagements in New York had now ceased and the Folk Group was shortly to return to London.

'*I guess Mike and I are not really suited*,' she wrote, '*and we want to go our separate ways after we get home.*

I thought we could get together again, you and I, Phil. I've got great ideas for us. Father kept us a bit old-fashioned, but all we need is a punk hairstyle and some really sinister-looking clothes, then we can get away with it. Not our usual stuff, of course, but something really new. We could do it. Can you get back to London and find us a flat? Too bad we sold all that stuff. We'll need a piano, too, for practice . . . two pianos, really. Can you see to that, Phil? Bless you . . . P.'

She had added a postscript.

'I'll tell you about what happened with Bryden Scott when I get home. Simon and I fell about laughing later. I knew he wouldn't turn you out when he looked into your big brown eyes. He's a big softie at heart . . . most men are, except ones like Mike Todd.'

Phil read the letter twice, then put it to one side. She would be furious with Patsy when she saw her, though she did offer one solution to their future.

But did she want that sort of life? She knew that she did not. It could never work for her, though if Patsy's ideas caught on, it might even mean an income reasonable enough to allow her to save for the future.

But she did not want to dye her hair green and pink, and she could imagine what Patsy meant by 'sinister' clothes. Suddenly Phil was laughing. Even if they quarrelled frequently and she did not always see eye to eye with her sister, Patsy could make her laugh. But she would definitely have something to say to her sister for hitting Bryden's car then sending her up here on the tissue of lies she had invented. She would certainly have something to say to Patsy about *that*.

Phil looked again at the scrawled handwriting, and suddenly she felt older than Patsy. Her sister had always taken the lead, but that was now over. Patsy would never lie to her again.

11

BRYDEN frowned when Phil refused to go to the Meet at Highfield.

"I don't like hunting," she said. "I just don't want to go."

"It isn't as bad as you think," he told her. "For the most part, the fox gets away. It's more of a social occasion now where the local people gather together and catch up to date with all that's been happening in the community. I understood you were helping Delia."

"Not any more, and you can't make me. I'm under notice to leave now."

This time the frown went very deep.

"That's uncalled for, Philomena. I wouldn't dream of forcing you to go against your will, and I know you will carry on here in your usual way until Miss Grant returns. But I understood you would wish to please Simon Browne."

"I am *not* going to marry Simon," she said, angrily. "I wish everyone would understand that. Simon docs now."

She heard him catch his breath, then he turned to her with obvious relief in his eyes.

"You're not . . . ?"

"No, I tried to say so all along. I only wished you would all listen to me."

"I'm very glad, my dear. I don't think it would have been suitable."

"Because of Barbara, you mean." Phil's anger was still burning brightly. Now all her pent-up emotions seemed to be washing over her so that she did not care what she said.

Immediately he was very still, then he swung round to stare at her.

"What has Browne been telling you?"

"Nothing. It wasn't Simon!"

She could have bitten out her tongue again as his eyes raked her face. How easy it was to allow things to slip one's tongue.

"Mrs Cleland," he said, softly. "It could only be Mrs Cleland."

"She only told me for the best. *Please* don't be angry with her. She only told me so that I would understand how . . . how you felt about Simon. I'm so sorry he hurt you because of . . of your wife. It must have been terrible for you."

"You don't know anything about it," he said, very quietly. "If Mrs Cleland told you, then you know nothing, because *she* knows nothing. And I do *not* like you gossiping with the servants. I accept that Mrs Cleland's motives are of the best. They always are. But do not think you know all the answers and all about my life just because my housekeeper has kept you informed."

"No. I . . . I'm sorry," she whispered.

It must all have been a great deal more harrowing than she imagined, and she longed to put her arms around him and comfort him. But she could not comfort Bryden. Perhaps no one could . . . except Delia? Could he find new happiness with Delia?

★ ★ ★

After Bryden had gone, Phil tidied up the last of her work. All the extra filing she had undertaken was now up to date and she hoped that Miss Grant would be pleased to have a reasonably good start when she resumed her work the following Monday week. One more week, then all would be finished for Phil at Murdo Cragg.

She had mentioned to Mrs Cleland that she would require to buy extra cases when she went shopping in Keswick, and the housekeeper had found an elderly trunk which was no longer in use.

"It was mine, Miss Phil, so we're robbing nobody," she said. "I had it when I came here, but Mrs Barbara gave me a set of cases for my Christmas, and I don't need this any longer. It would save your money. Oh dear, I'm really sorry you're going. You've brought this old house to life again, what with your piano playing and your nice bright voice talking and laughing all over the house."

She had not been doing much laughing recently, thought Phil.

"I'll miss it, too, Mrs Cleland," she said, sadly.

She had counted up her money with Patsy's letter in mind, but she would have difficulty in finding anywhere to rent now with the money she had in hand. She hoped Patsy would not arrive home stony-broke.

Phil was sorting through bundles of books and music to put in her trunk when the telephone shrilled and she hurried back downstairs. It was a call from Bryden's agent.

"I'm sorry but Mr Scott is out at the moment," she apologised. "Can I take a message, Mr Lunn?"

"Hold on."

Geoffrey Lunn spoke for a moment away from the telephone, then his voice sounded again.

"Could you possibly contact him for me, Miss Blake? It's rather urgent. I might have some news for him regarding a possible new television series. I'm at a meeting now . . . "

"How long would I have, Mr Lunn?"

"I shall be here for another thirty minutes, Miss Blake . . . maybe not quite that long . . . "

"I'll try to find him for you, Mr Lunn."

Swiftly she dialled Highfield's telephone number but the housekeeper told her that Mr Scott was out with the others at the Hunt.

"Up in the fells behind Highfield, Miss Blake," she said, helpfully.

Phil ran out into the yard, but there was only the pony and trap available, and hardly stopping to think, she hitched them up as she had seen Donald Douglas do so many times, then sprang into the small trap and moments later she was guiding the pony towards the narrow road which led over the fells. Somehow she must attract Bryden's attention, and if he saw the pony and trap, he would surely ride towards her.

It seemed hours before Phil heard the baying of the hounds as she turned the trap along the narrow mountain road. In the distance she could see the riders strewn out along the fells with the baying hounds running furiously, and she reined in to see how best to attract Bryden's attention. Some of the riders wore pink coats, but for the most part they wore ordinary riding dress, including Bryden.

"I only go to make a social occasion of it," he told Phil, but she had not softened in her own attitude.

Suddenly her pony whinnied, and Phil's eye was caught by a movement along the hedge, and a moment later she saw that it was a large dog fox, its coat wet after crossing a small beck nearby. No doubt it had thrown the hounds off the scent, thought Phil, as she and the animal stared at one another. It was too exhausted for fear, and its golden eyes blazed balefully, as she slid out of the trap.

Swiftly stripping off her sheepskin jacket, Phil slowly walked forward, then quickly dropped it over the creature as it tried to leap into life once more. It struggled but a moment later she had bundled it up, using every ounce of strength, and had placed it in the trap where it lay quiet once more. Momentarily her errand to Bryden was forgotten as she turned the trap and started out once again for Murdo Cragg. The animal lay limply within the confines of Phil's thick coat.

But what should she do with it? she wondered desperately. All she knew was that she must hide it until the hunt was over. Tales came into her head, in particular the tale of how a fox had killed three hounds by luring them over a cliff, which was Delia's favourite story, but more particularly about how a farmer had carried a fox, slung across his shoulders, all the way home after it had been run to ground and declared dead. He had saved it from destruction in order to adorn his wife's new coat, but when he threw the creature down near the farmhouse in order to climb a fence, it was only to find the animal running smartly across the field when he turned to pick it up. They were wily, and clever, and only the old and the sick were caught. Well, *this* one could well be old, thought Phil, as she guided the pony towards home, but it was not going to be caught.

She was driving badly again, and she remembered that she had been forbidden to take the pony and trap out by herself. Then from behind she heard the hounds once more, and yelled at the pony to pick up more speed.

Phil's fear was great as they thundered along the narrow mountain road back to Murdo Cragg, then suddenly she was aware of a horseman behind her, and of someone shouting her name, but she could not tell if it were Bryden or Simon. She could hear the hounds baying dismally, and her one thought was to make the fox safe. It could stay in an outhouse for the present. She would lock it into the boar-pen.

Phil was barely conscious of stopping and bundling her burden into the boar-pen. It had a very low doorway and she forgot to stoop and knocked her head as she walked in, after unlocking the door. Then, suddenly the world was spinning around her and Bryden was galloping into the yard as she staggered away from relocking the door and stood, swaying, in the cobbled yard. Delia and Simon Browne followed close behind him.

"Have you gone quite mad?" Delia was asking, shrilly.

Phil tried to shake her head, then suddenly Bryden had slipped off his horse and was catching her in his arms.

"Ring your agent," she muttered. "Telephone call for you . . . urgent . . . "

She was muttering incoherently, trying

211

to clear her head of pain. She felt cold and clammy inside and her simple sweater was no protection against the cold wind which was blowing off the fells. She was shivering inside and out.

"Not even a decent anorak on her," Delia was saying with disgust. "Where's that old sheepskin coat she always wears?"

Bryden was forcing some brandy between her lips as Simon appeared and Delia turned to him, both of them now having dismounted.

"We'd better get back, Simon," she said, angrily. "Bryden isn't our only guest, and this girl is not a guest at all. Trust her to do her best to ruin our day. She's out of her mind. Anyway, we have to see to the others."

"Is she hurt?" Simon was asking. "What's it all about anyway?"

Phil's teeth were now chattering with nerves and her head ached abominably, making her feel sick.

"Telephone call . . . to your agent," she said, more clearly. "Important. I had to come to find you . . . thought you would see the trap . . . "

"Is *that* all?" asked Bryden.

"And she spoils our day for that," said Delia. "Heaven knows where the hounds are now, and we'll never raise another fox. Come on, Simon. Are you coming, Bryden? Mrs Cleland can see to the girl. Thank God Heather Grant is coming back, and we'll all be back to normal. Maybe you don't think you did any harm, Miss Blake, but you forced us to come after you to see you were okay, driving like a maniac. I was certain you were out of control."

"Come on, Delia, you've said enough," said Simon. "Let's go home."

He looked at Phil whose eyes had now filled with tears.

"Delia was right," he said, sadly. "You would never have fitted in at Highfield. It would have been a mistake. Good luck, Phil."

Bryden carried her in and settled her on to the couch as he had done the first time they met, then he went off to look for some tissues.

"My head hurts," she whispered, and he explored it with his fingers. "I forgot about the doorway."

"My God!"

The tears flowed faster.

"And . . . and the fox is in the boar-pen . . . wrapped in my sheepskin coat," she managed, almost choking on the words. "He was exhausted and resting in a ditch near a hedge. The telephone, Bryden . . . urgent . . . "

She felt very sick and everything was whirling about her as she fainted.

★ ★ ★

When Phil came round she found herself lying on the large settle and Mrs Cleland was poking up the fire nearby.

"I . . . I still feel sick," she said.

Her head was thumping and she tried to sit up.

"I expect you do, Miss Phil," the housekeeper said, grimly. "There now,

214

you should feel better after you've had a sip of this."

She held a glass to Phil's lips and the girl drank, then coughed. She lay back, allowing things to settle and fighting off the hot tears. Everything reminded her so much of the first day she had come to Murdo Cragg, when she had lain weak and exhausted with hunger on this very same settle. They had been kind to her then, Bryden and Mrs Cleland, just as they were being kind to her now.

But Bryden must be feeling very angry with her, and no doubt the Brownes were furious. She had probably made them all look ridiculous, and herself most of all. Yet she had done it all on impulse, and she knew that if she could save the fox again, she would try to do it in exactly the same way.

At one of the farms she had been shown the ravages made by a fox when it got into the chicken run, but she had blamed the farmer in that particular case. They were careless people who left fences unmended, then complained when their cattle strayed. No doubt the state of the chicken run had been an open invitation to the fox. At the same time, it had grieved her that the animal had killed all the hens even if it only needed one to appease its hunger.

"They have to be kept down," Bryden had told her, "just like deer have to be culled. Man has to help Nature a little."

"But not this way," she had said, shivering. "Surely it ought to be left to the gamekeeper."

"Is Bryden very angry?" she asked Mrs Cleland.

"He's not too pleased about something," the housekeeper admitted, "and I came in for a few sharp words, too, Miss Phil."

"Oh . . . I'm sorry," she mumbled. "I didn't mean to let the cat out of the bag. He . . . he guessed."

"Och, don't worry about that. We've had our differences before, Mr Bryden and I. He usually wins, but only when

I let him. Now put this blanket on, lass. You gave yourself a bad knock on the head. The doctor is coming to look you over."

"There's no need for that!" cried Phil, trying to struggle to her feet.

But again she felt sick and giddy, and a moment later she was being pushed rather unceremoniously on to the settle, and Bryden was towering over her.

"Lie still!" he commanded. "Haven't you given me enough to worry about already? Stay there until Dr Murchison arrives, then we'll see what you've done to yourself."

"What happened? . . . about the fox, I mean?"

A grim smile played about his mouth.

"Your coat is being sent to the cleaner's. Oh, he's gone, no doubt to savage a few more chickens, but your conscience can be clear. You saved his life."

She stared back at him miserably.

"And I love you for it," he added,

and she had to force back the tears. She wished he would not be so kind to her.

"Did you telephone Mr Lunn?" she asked.

"I did, and he had good news for me. We plan to do a series for a children's programme. I have also been offered a lecture tour of the U.S.A."

"Oh, that . . . that's wonderful," said Phil, and hoped she sounded as happy as she ought to feel for him. But it seemed like the final straw for her. When she returned to London, she would never see him again.

"Philomena, I want to talk to you," he began, but a moment later Mrs Cleland knocked on the door to tell them Dr Murchison had arrived. He examined her carefully, peering into her eyes and taking her blood pressure.

"I reckon you'll live, young lady, if you don't make a habit of knocking yourself about. You need to take things easy, though, for a day or two."

He departed and Phil waited for

Bryden to return. No doubt he had made arrangements for her to be taken to London.

But it was later in the evening before he came to talk to her again, and she found out that it was for an entirely different reason.

12

"HOW do you feel?" asked Bryden, as he came to sit beside Phil in the drawing room. She'd had a light meal on a tray and Mrs Cleland had helped her to the bathroom where she had soaked in a bath which smelled of rose petals. Now she wore a soft creamy-coloured hostess gown with green and gold braid at the neck and on the loose-fitting sleeves. She had brushed her short hair into soft curls and she felt warm and comfortable.

Mrs Cleland had tucked a soft mohair rug about her knees and had found her a few of her favourite Scottish magazines which were keeping Phil entertained.

"Can you lay those aside for a moment?" Bryden asked, irritably.

"Of course," she laughed. "Mrs

Cleland thinks the television will give me a headache."

"Have you got a headache?"

"Not much now. I could be back to work tomorrow."

"Oh, never mind work," he said, crossly. "Philomena, we've got to talk. I've got to know where I stand. Are you quite sure you do not want to marry Simon Browne? Maybe he and I don't get along, but he . . . well . . . perhaps I have no right to try to influence you."

"I have never loved Simon," she said, quietly. "I thought I did a long time ago, but I soon found out my mistake. Oh, he's all right really, and will no doubt settle down with a girl who understands him and his way of life, but it won't be me. I'd rather go back to London and start working again with Patsy."

He looked at her keenly. "What's all this?"

She explained about Patsy's letter and he listened carefully, then got up to walk about.

"Is that what you really want to do then, Philomena? Maybe you could be a big star one day."

She was shaking her head. "I doubt if Patsy and I will see eye to eye. I don't want to dye my hair and wear black leather, but I could maybe compromise a little, if Patsy will, too. We'll make out. There's no need for you to worry about me or . . . or feel responsible for me."

"I can't help worrying about you, damn it," he said. "You might as well know that I've been foolish enough to fall in love with you, Philomena." He was silent for a moment and she felt too stunned to speak. He loved her! Bryden loved her! But . . . but what about his Wild Poppy?

"I know I'm too old for you."

"Oh, but you're not too old," she said, quickly. "Oh no, you're not. I mean, if . . . if you really *do* love me, because I love you, too, you see, only I always thought it was Delia or . . . or maybe even your wife still. I . . . I never thought it was me."

He had come to sit down beside her, and suddenly she was in his arms and he was kissing her wildly. Phil's heart hammered and her whole body began to tremble with happiness.

Then as suddenly, Bryden was pushing her away.

"No, I'd better tell you everything, then you can decide. You see, I . . . I feel responsible for the death of my wife and the baby. It was no one else's fault. It was mine. Mrs Cleland was wrong when she told you I blamed Simon Browne."

His face had grown white and pinched and Phil saw, again, the look of unhappiness and strain which she had always connected with herself.

"I should not have married Barbara," he said, "only I fell in love with her. I loved her very much, Philomena. But my home is here at Murdo Cragg, as is my life's work, and she only wanted to live in London. For a while we did and Barbara and I had an almost feverish round of gaiety. I found it very tiring, and I'm sure she did, too, so that when she was expecting Lee, her health was not very good. I . . . I *insisted* that we came home to Murdo Cragg."

He rubbed a hand across his forehead.

"When Lee was born, the doctor warned us that she was . . . was not a normal baby. She was handicapped. There was brain damage. But Barbara refused to accept that any child of hers could be handicapped. She, herself, was so beautiful, you see. She used to live so feverishly, as though to prove to herself, and to me, that she was perfect physically. I tried to tell her that Lee's handicap was just one of those tragedies which can happen to people. I felt that if I built up a life for her at Murdo Cragg, then she might grow up a happy child. I would get all the help for her I could.

"But we had to keep these worries to ourselves at Barbara's insistence. So far Lee looked like an ordinary child, but for her eyes, and the fact that she was so quiet."

Phil wanted to hold him, but Bryden was once again pacing the floor.

"My work was becoming better known, and I had earned money with my television programmes. I had brought up my small family of squirrels and they caught people's imagination, but I did not foresee that it would bring people here to . . . to look at us. Barbara hated that. It . . . it was she who killed little Betsy. She was not killed accidentally by one of the visitors as people believed. I never allowed her, or anyone else, to know that I knew the truth. I saw her, you see . . . but it was too late then. Betsy was dead. I . . . I think I hated Barbara at that moment."

"Oh, Bryden!" said Phil, shocked, and he turned a white face to her.

"I know. After that, it all happened so quickly. Simon Browne came home from university, and Barbara encouraged him to take her out. He was old for his years, and she looked very young and beautiful. They used to go dancing together. But I was afraid people would talk so I remonstrated with her. And I think Colonel Browne had a word with Simon. He agreed to go to London. Then the following week, Lee was ill and when the doctor came, we talked to him, Barbara and I. He said Lee would never be well. I should have seen how upset Barbara was, but I didn't. A day or two later she took Lee out in our old car which needed servicing, and the rest you know. But all my life I must ask myself if it was an accident, or . . . or . . . ?"

Again he was silent.

"It was my fault. I should have looked after her better, and I should have had that car checked. That's why I could not let you drive your Mini away from here when you first came. I couldn't let it happen to another girl, especially a small waif of a child who soon wormed her way into my heart! As soon as I really *looked* at that car, then at you, I knew I had to keep you with me."

"Even after Patsy?"

"I've met lots of Patsys, but only one Philomena. I love you, my dear, but I have no right to that love."

"Oh, Bryden, please don't say that," she cried. "Haven't you punished yourself enough? It was a great tragedy in your life, but you . . . we . . . *we* must put it behind us now. Don't you see that you would be punishing both of us if you refuse to take the happiness offered to *both* of us now? The only thing is, I . . . I'm not really good enough for you. I mean, I'm not anybody really . . . "

"Not anybody!" he cried. "What nonsense! You are a beautiful, talented girl and I love you. You can tell your sister she must carry on making her own way with her music, just as she did when she walked out on you. I wanted you to have an older relative to whom I could explain myself. I don't want to take advantage of your youth and sweetness. You're like a lovely primrose in that gown."

Bryden took her in his arms and kissed her passionately, and Phil's heart sang with happiness when she saw the strain in him beginning to ease. It might be some time before Bryden was completely better, but she had made a good start.

"I always did love primroses," he was saying.

Phil's hand gently touched his hair. Perhaps now he would think about his Wild Poppy with a gentler, softer love, but if *she* could keep him now, she would settle for that.

THE END

WITH SOMEBODY ELSE
Theresa Charles

Rosamond sets off for Cornwall with Hugo to meet his family, blissfully unaware of the shocks in store for her.

A SUMMER FOR STRANGERS
Claire Hamilton

Because she had lost her job, her flat and she had no money, Tabitha agreed to pose as Adam's future wife although she believed the scheme to be deceitful and cruel.

VILLA OF SINGING WATER
Angela Petron

The disquieting incidents that occurred at the Vatican and the Colosseum did not trouble Jan at first, but then they became increasingly unpleasant and alarming.

DOCTOR NAPIER'S NURSE
Pauline Ash

When cousins Midge and Derry are entered as probationer nurses on the same day but at different hospitals they agree to exchange identities.

A GIRL LIKE JULIE
Louise Ellis

Caroline absolutely adored Hugh Barrington, but then Julie Crane came into their lives. Julie was the kind of girl who attracts men without even trying.

COUNTRY DOCTOR
Paula Lindsay

When Evan Richmond bought a practice in a remote country village he did not realise that a casual encounter would lead to the loss of his heart.

ENCORE
Helga Moray

Craig and Janet realise that their true happiness lies with each other, but it is only under traumatic circumstances that they can be reunited.

NICOLETTE
Ivy Preston

When Grant Alston came back into her life, Nicolette was faced with a dilemma. Should she follow the path of duty or the path of love?

THE GOLDEN PUMA
Margaret Way

Catherine's time was spent looking after her father's Queensland farm. But what life was there without David, who wasn't interested in her?

HOSPITAL BY THE LAKE
Anne Durham

Nurse Marguerite Ingleby was always ready to become personally involved with her patients, to the despair of Brian Field, the Senior Surgical Registrar, who loved her.

VALLEY OF CONFLICT
David Farrell

Isolated in a hostel in the French Alps, Ann Russell sees her fiancé being seduced by a young girl. Then comes the avalanche that imperils their lives.

NURSE'S CHOICE
Peggy Gaddis

A proposal of marriage from the incredibly handsome and wealthy Reagan was enough to upset any girl — and Brooke Martin was no exception.

A DANGEROUS MAN
Anne Goring

Photographer Polly Burton was on safari in Mombasa when she met enigmatic Leon Hammond. But unpredictability was the name of the game where Leon was concerned.

PRECIOUS INHERITANCE
Joan Moules

Karen's new life working for an authoress took her from Sussex to a foreign airstrip and a kidnapping; to a real life adventure as gripping as any in the books she typed.

VISION OF LOVE
Grace Richmond

When Kathy takes over the rundown country kennels she finds Alec Stinton, a local vet, very helpful. But their friendship arouses bitter jealousy and a tragedy seems inevitable.